BY WATT KEY

Alabama Moon
Dirt Road Home
Fourmile

WATT KEY

FARRAR STRAUS GIROUX
NEW YORK

Farrar Straus Giroux Books for Young Readers
175 Fifth Avenue, New York 10010

Distributed in Canada by D&M Publishers, Inc.
Printed in the United States of America
by RR Donnelley & Sons Company, Harrisonburg, Virginia
Designed by Andrew Arnold
First edition, 2012
1   3   5   7   9   10   8   6   4   2

mackids.com

Library of Congress Cataloging-in-Publication Data
Key, Watt.
    Fourmile / Watt Key. — 1st ed.
        p.   cm.
    Summary: "A mysterious stranger arrives at a boy's rundown Alabama
farm home, just as a dangerous situation is unfolding for the twelve-
year-old and his widowed mother" — Provided by publisher.
    ISBN 978-0-374-35095-6 (hardcover)
    ISBN 978-0-374-32441-4 (e-book)
    [1. Fathers and sons—Fiction.   2. Violence—Fiction.   3. Farm
life—Alabama—Fiction.   4. Alabama—Fiction.]   1. Title.   II. Title:
Four mile.

PZ7.K516Fo 2012
[Fic]—dc23
                                                              2012003220

For Adele and Mary Michael:
Stick together

1

heard Mother calling, but I didn't answer. I lay in the scattered hay and stared at the afternoon sunbeams angling through the big bay doors of the barn. Against the wall were damp, moldy bales that had been in the same place for over a year. They smelled more of wet dirt and decay than anything fresh-cut. Two sheets of tin had blown off the roof during the winter and the place was rotting. There was too much to do now. Mother and I couldn't keep up.

I rolled over and faced my dog, Joe. He lifted his chin and nosed the chewed-up stick lying in front of him.

"Not right now," I said.

Joe rested his chin on the ground again. He was patient.

"Foster!" Mother called again.

I stood and walked into the sunbeams with Joe

following. I stopped just outside and looked across the yard at her. She'd known where I was, but she wouldn't come after me. She didn't like the barn now. She said there was nothing we could do about it.

"Dax's here!" she called. "Come get washed up before dinner!"

I looked over the rail fence at the pasture beyond. The cows had been gone for several months, sold to the farmer behind us. Johnsongrass grew waist-high, looking like something that would be a giant briar patch in another year. Daddy's farm truck and Kubota tractor sat under the shed. The place had grown still and quiet and lifeless. There was nothing we could do about any of it.

I left Joe waiting at the back door and stepped into the kitchen. Mother was pulling a baked chicken from the oven and I smelled her perfume over the roasted meat. I never knew her to wear perfume until Dax Ganey started coming around. The smell of it made me queasy.

He leaned against the sink, working a can of old Milwaukee beer like it was hinged on his hand, watching her. It seemed he was always leaning on something, skinny and hungry-looking. He wore his blue work pants and white button-down shirt that said RIVIERA UTILITIES on the pocket. He was nearly five years younger than her and wore his hair long in the back, sometimes pulling it into a ponytail. Mother said she'd met him about two months before when he was surveying an underground power line in front of our house. The first time she'd had him over to eat I thought he was as cool and smooth as a movie star. Gradually I came to realize how he really was when Mother wasn't looking. The only thing I liked about Dax was that he worked most evenings during the week. Since Mother worked at the post office during the day, Saturdays and Sundays were about the only time I had to see him.

Dax flicked the last swallow of beer into the sink and dropped the empty into the trash. Then he turned to me and studied me until I looked away. He wouldn't smile unless Mother was watching him.

"How you doin', Foster?" he said.

I started past him. "Fine," I said.

I heard the oven door shut and sensed Mother's eyes on me. "Shake his hand, Foster," she said.

I stopped next to him and held out my hand without looking at him. He had a snake tattoo on the bottom of his wrist. I didn't like shaking his hand. I didn't mind the tattoo, but his fingers were strong like cables and he usually squeezed my knuckles until it hurt, like he wanted to warn me of something.

This time his hand was limp and clammy.

"Look a man in the eyes when you shake his hand, son," he said cheerfully.

I didn't. I pulled away and started to my room.

"What'd *I* do?" I heard him say.

"You didn't do anything, Dax." Mother sighed.

I went into my room, shut the door, and rubbed my hand. I could still hear them.

"Why's he hang out in the barn?"

"I don't know," she said, like she was tired of thinking about it.

I stood in the middle of the floor, holding a clean shirt, staring at my closet.

"Maybe I'll take him fishin' with me. Might snap him out of it."

I changed shirts and stood before my mirror, still listening, but wishing I wasn't.

"I need to get him off this farm," she said. "Get him in a neighborhood with other kids. We've got to sell this place."

"Where does that leave me, sweetie?" he said smoothly.

"Stop that, Dax."

"Stop what?"

"You know what. Go in there and watch television and give me time to get this together."

I waited until I heard another beer can snap, then I forced myself into the bathroom to wash my hands.

I walked into the kitchen and Mother turned from the sink and inspected me.

"I wish you'd put on some clean trousers."

"*He* didn't change."

She turned back to the sink. I noticed where her apron parted in the back that she had on a dress I'd only seen her wear on Sundays when we used to go to church.

"Okay," I said.

"Thank you for doing that," she replied. "And I'd like it if you'd go sit in the living room with Mr. Ganey and keep him company."

After I put on clean pants I went into the living room and sat in the club chair across from him. He didn't look at me or say anything. He was more interested in a rerun of *Walker, Texas Ranger*. I took the opportunity to study the side of his face. He reminded me of a goat. A smooth-shaved goat. Restless and jumpy with eyes that blinked too much, like whatever went on inside his head was too fast for the face that held it. He shot a look at me and I glanced away.

"You like Chuck Norris?" he asked.

"I don't know," I said.

In my periphery I saw him turn back to the television.

"What do you do out in the barn?" he asked.

"Nothing."

Neither of us said anything for a minute.

"What's wrong with that dog of yours?"

"Nothing's wrong with him."

"I about had to kick the crap out of it last time I came over here."

I didn't answer him.

"You need to put him on a rope."

"He never bit anybody."

"He about started on me."

I didn't respond.

"Your momma says you been givin' her trouble."

I stared at my hands.

"Says you been gettin' in fights at school."

I looked at him. I couldn't believe she'd told him about it. He turned to me again and I looked away at the television. Then he was chuckling to himself. "Kid needs to get in a few fights. Get over the fear of it early. You don't wanna grow up and be a pansy-ass, do you?"

I shook my head. I just wanted him to stop talking.

"But let me tell you somethin'," he said.

Mother walked in before he could tell me anything and I let out a breath I didn't know I'd been holding.

"Dinner is served, you two," she said proudly.

I got up quickly and started for the dining room table. I didn't like being alone with him. Dax scared me in a way that I didn't understand. In a way that I'd never felt. Like somebody I'd find standing over my bed at night, closing those fingers around my throat.

2

Good chicken," Dax said, wiping his mouth with a napkin.

"Thank you," Mother said.

I stared at my peas. I wasn't hungry. I wanted to go back out to the barn.

"I might take some of this home with me," he said.

She smiled at him and I hated him more.

"Mr. Ganey said he might take you fishing, Foster."

I didn't answer.

"Foster?" she said.

I looked at her. I could see him chewing and watching.

"Did you hear me?" she asked.

"Yes, ma'am."

"What do you think about that?"

"I don't want to go fishing."

"You used to love to fish."

"Daddy loved to fish. I liked to go with him."

I saw she was getting nervous by the way the side of her mouth started to twitch.

"Maybe another time," Dax said.

Mother hesitated, then looked at her plate and lifted another bite.

Dax took a gulp of beer and set the can down again. "You know, if you'd fix this place up a little, it might sell."

Mother looked at him with a pained expression.

"What?" he said. "I'm talkin' about that barn out there and the fence and the crap in the yard. People see that stuff."

"I can't afford all that, Dax."

"Then how you expect to get the kind of money you want for it?"

"The real estate person said we could sell it as is."

"Real estate people are whores for a contract too."

"Dax," she said, glancing at me.

"You don't think he's heard that before? He's almost thirteen years old. He's heard a lot more than that."

"Why don't you help her?" I said to my plate.

He turned to me. "Help her what?"

"Fix the place up. You come over here enough."

"Foster," Mother said.

"You gettin' smart with me, boy?"

I faced him. "You could help her if you wanted. But you don't want to."

"Foster!" Mother snapped, putting her fork down.

Dax wouldn't take his eyes off me and I turned away. "Don't think I ain't man enough in your life to put a belt to your ass," he said.

"Dax, that's enough," Mother said.

I stared at my plate, breathing hard. I wanted to say something, but I didn't know what. She was taking his side. My face was hot with anger and fear and confusion. I pushed back from the table and stood.

"Sit down, Foster," she said.

I turned and headed for the front door. My head was screaming.

"Your momma said to sit down," he called after me.

But I kept on. Out the door and into the driveway until I was standing before his Chevy S10 pickup. I heard Dax pushing his chair back as I knelt and pulled a brick from the flower bed lining.

"Leave him alone, Dax," Mother said.

"Hey!" he shouted after me.

I hurled the brick at his windshield where it made a crunching sound like a foot in wet gravel. The glass spiderwebbed and the brick bounced off and skipped across the hood.

"Son of a—!" I heard him yell. I stood there, shaking, staring at it. Suddenly his hand slammed into the back of my neck and I stiffened against it. I tried to drop to my knees, but he held me there, squeezing so I couldn't move. Joe bolted around the corner of the house, a white blur, growling with rage. Dax shoved me into him and leaped onto the hood of the truck. I fell over Joe's back and both of us went down. The dog squirmed out from under me and leaped at Dax, barking and raking his toenails across the front grille like he wanted to tear him apart.

"Grab him, Foster!" I heard Mother yell from behind.

I got to my knees and crawled to Joe and grabbed him by the collar. I pulled him to me and held tight as he bucked and strained.

Dax was backed against the windshield with his heels on the wipers. "What the hell, Linda!" he shouted.

I struggled with Joe until I was finally able to stand and drag him toward the backyard.

"Foster!" I heard Mother yelling behind me. "Put him up and get back out here!"

3

That night Mother asked me to apologize to Dax. I stayed silent and she sent me to my room. I lay there and listened to them arguing.

"What am I supposed to do about that windshield, Linda?" he said. "That's prob'ly a three-hundred-dollar piece of glass. I got to go to work in that truck!"

"I'll pay for it, Dax."

"Yeah? Where you gonna get three hundred dollars?"

"I'll pay for it," she said again.

"Gonna cost another couple hundred to take the dents out of the hood."

"That's fine," she said. "Whatever it costs."

"Work it out of his ass," he said. "What the hell's wrong with him?"

"Please, Dax," she said.

Neither one of them spoke for a moment.

"I'm gonna kick the stew out of that ugly dog," he finally said. "Then I'm gonna kill him."

"Just sit down, Dax. I'll get a beer for you."

"Shoot the damn thing."

"Let's go outside," she said.

"Let's go to a bar."

"I don't want to go to a bar," she said.

"Fine. I'm goin' by myself. Get my beer."

There was a period of silence before I heard the front door shut. Then more silence. Finally I saw the shadows of her feet pass my bedroom and heard her door close and heard her crying.

Sunday morning Mother was quieter than usual. I still wasn't sorry for throwing the brick, but I felt miserable that I'd upset her. We ate breakfast with barely a word and then she told me we were going to Dax's house to apologize.

Neither of us had been to his house before. She looked up his address in the phone book and wrote it down and we got into her Honda Accord and set out. It was about a fifteen-minute drive. After several miles of country road we passed through Robertsdale, a small farming community marked by a single caution light. A few miles outside of town we passed a metal fabrication shop with a yard full of new and repaired Dumpsters. Just after that we came to a red clay road with a plywood sign that read GANEY TAXIDERMY.

"What's taxidermy?" I asked.

"Mounting deer heads and things," she said. "He told me he does it on the side."

We traveled the dirt road about a mile between walls of pine plantation until we came to the first break in the trees. There was a five-acre cutout surrounded by a hog wire fence. A small white one-level, vinyl-sided house sat near the back of the lot. Another GANEY TAXIDERMY sign was nailed to a fence post near the road. I didn't see his truck and felt relief wash over me.

"I don't think he's home," I said.

She turned in to the driveway. "He said he has a shop behind the house. He might be back there."

Dread rushed over me again.

The driveway wasn't paved. Nothing more than dirt tracks up to and around the house. We drove through the side yard and saw his truck before a small, unpainted cinder-block building with a steel door and metal roof.

When I got out I noticed how quiet it was. Other than a few crows calling, the pine plantation seemed to absorb everything. The smell of turpentine and stink bugs was heavy in the air.

"Dax!" she called.

There was no answer.

She stepped toward the door and knocked on it. "Dax!" she called again.

I wondered why she didn't just open it, but I wasn't about to encourage her.

Suddenly the door swung in and he was standing there with his goat face, wiping his hands on his jeans. His thighs were smeared with blood. His arms were covered with it up to his elbows. He wore a white V-neck undershirt that was specked with red splotches and flecked with pieces of meat and jelly fat. I saw the shock in Mother's face.

He studied her for a second, then glanced at me and back at her. "Hey," he said.

"Hi," she said. "I hope you don't mind us coming by."

He seemed to think about it. Finally he backed up a few steps. "Come on in," he said.

The room was cluttered with stuffed animals—deer heads, fox squirrels, a bobcat, two coyotes. It was cold and smelled like blood and urine and animal fat. Against the right wall were three white deep-freeze coolers. Above them were shelves stacked with mold inserts of animal body parts. A window unit droned against the rear wall. Beneath it was a large stainless-steel sink and countertop with the carcass of some animal turned inside out and a skinning knife lying across it. The wet cement floor sloped to a drain in the center.

Dax walked to the table and picked up the knife. He put

his back to us and began scraping at the hide. "Workin' on a boar for a friend of mine," he said.

Something about the gore of the place and the dead animals was both fascinating and frightening at the same time. I looked at Mother and saw the nervous twitch she got at the side of her mouth.

"Foster has something to tell you," she said.

She looked at me.

"I'm sorry about the brick," I said.

He kept scraping.

"He's going to work it off," she said.

He still didn't face us. "I tell you what, boy," he said, "one of these days you're gonna appreciate what it takes to earn a livin' and buy somethin' like a truck."

I didn't respond. He set the knife down and faced us and leaned against the counter. "You hear me?"

"Yes, sir."

He studied me for a second, then turned back to the animal hide. Mother reached into her pocket and pulled out an envelope and walked over to him. She started to reach around him and set it on the counter, but changed her mind and tucked it into his back pocket. Then she touched his shoulder with her hand. "Let me know if it's not enough," she said.

He kept working. She hesitated for a moment, then pulled her hand away. "I'll call you later," she said.

4

Granddaddy was driving down from Montgomery for lunch. I waited for him with Joe under the pecan tree closest to the house. This tree was bigger and older than the rest, offset like it had never been part of the orchard at all. Daddy once said he thought it had been there since before the land was cleared for farming. Sometimes I liked to imagine it long ago in the midst of a thick forest. I remembered the first time I came to Fourmile when I was six and how small I felt standing under it.

It seemed strange that we were moving down near the Alabama coast to have a farm, but Daddy said it was everything he'd been looking for and the price was too good to pass up. He'd worked and saved ten years for it as a UPS driver in Montgomery. His childhood was spent on a cattle farm in Mississippi and he knew the business. Mother had always been supportive of his dream, but it certainly made it easier that she was already familiar with Baldwin County from having spent a few summers there as a child.

It was late fall when we left the Montgomery suburbs and headed south. After two hours we exited the interstate and drove east into the country. The blacktop was faded and worn and gouged by plow points. There was so little traffic that the road stayed sprinkled with leaves that crinkled like paper under the car tires and whorled behind and resettled. Eventually we came to a pecan orchard and just past it was a rusty metal sign that read FOURMILE. The dirt drive ran the outside edge of the orchard up to the house. We got out and I stood under the pecan trees and before the expanse of open pastureland. The air was cool and clean and still. The countryside was soft and quiet, punctuated with the lowing of cows and the whistling of killdeer and doves. The smell of hay and damp soil and soybeans flowed into my nose.

Fourmile wasn't very big compared to other farms in the area. Just the ten-acre orchard and two hundred acres of pasture that backed up to another sixty acres of creek bottom. The house was a one-level brick ranch with three bedrooms. In addition to the barn and the tractor shed there was a cattle chute and a dipping trough. Our closest neighbor was a widow a mile to the north.

I don't remember much about my father before we came to the farm. He was at work most of the time and when he was home he always seemed tired. He never seemed tired after we came to Fourmile. There was always something to do, something he wanted to show or teach me.

In fall we woke before school and crouched at the edge of the pasture and shot doves as they whistled in through the slanted sunbeams, their wings still heavy with dew. In winter I sat with him just inside the trees of the creek bottom, our breath misting before us, waiting for the eight-point buck he called Walter. And when the heat of an Alabama summer threatened to bake us dry, Mother made picnics and he drove us up the blacktop to Tillman's bridge, where we soaked in the clear creek water.

As I grew older he taught me about using tools and working on equipment and tending the livestock. I looked forward to waking early and feeding the cows. I lay in bed at night thinking about the projects we'd planned, like the new watering system and the hay feeder. Work and play and attention that makes a boy proud and confident and secure.

Fourmile was a life we built together, something I was molded around, all I knew, the best of him and me and Mother. As if leaving it wasn't enough to bear, I had to watch it die first.

———————

When Granddaddy pulled up in his big silver Buick sedan, I didn't see Grandmother with him. But I hadn't expected to. I knew this was a special trip.

His car came to a stop and he studied me and Joe out the window. "Fine spring day we've got here, you two."

He didn't know anything about farm life. I couldn't imagine him out of his leather lace-up shoes and Sunday suit and felt hat. His face was soft and calm and free of worries. I was ashamed of myself for letting him down.

I got up and approached the car. "Hey, Granddaddy."

"Looks like you grew another two inches on me," he replied. "Maybe you got some of your grandmother's side in you."

I looked at the ground and shrugged my shoulders. Sometimes he just said things like that when we both knew it wasn't true. It was obvious that I took after Daddy, thin, not overly tall, with hair that went from blond in the summer to brown in winter.

He got out and stretched and looked around. He still had a lot of energy and his eyes were always wide and wet with good nature.

"Your grandmomma said to tell you she's sorry she couldn't drive down. She's a little under the weather."

"That's okay. I hope she gets better."

"Oh, she'll be okay. Just a spring cold. Your mother inside?"

"Yes, sir."

He leaned back into his car and grabbed a newspaper off the seat. I saw that it was a copy of the *Montgomery Advertiser*. He tapped it against his leg. "Let's go check on her."

"Okay," I said. I was up for anything that put off the talk I knew he'd driven almost three hours to have with me.

5

Granddaddy said he wanted to take a drive to the coast and see a house he had rented for years when Mother was young.

"The old Morris place," he reminded her.

"I haven't been by there in twenty years," she said.

"We'll be back after a while."

We left her at the kitchen table, going through the newspaper, looking for houses she thought we could afford. She'd been doing the same thing for nearly eight months, ever since she'd told me that we were moving.

Granddaddy and I drove through the countryside with the windows down and the spring air cool and smelling of cut grass and pine sap. His car was big and comfortable and I sat back in the seat and wished he would tell me everything I needed to know about growing up. Surely he had the answers. Surely there would come a day when he would just laugh and tell me it was all a joke and give me the secrets.

"Your mother says you might need to make a little extra money."

"Yes, sir," I said.

"Thought about what you might do?"

I shrugged.

"Seems to me like there's a fence needs painting."

"It's a pretty big fence."

"You're a big kid now."

I didn't answer.

"House in the city doesn't require all this upkeep," he said.

"Have you met Dax?" I asked him.

He shook his head. "Haven't met him yet."

"I don't like him."

"That doesn't give you an excuse to damage his property."

"No, sir," I said, sinking lower in my seat.

He reached over into the glove compartment and pulled out a roll of Life Savers candy. He held them out to me and I shook my head.

"No?" he asked.

"No, thanks," I said.

He shrugged and stuck one in his mouth and worked it slowly in his cheek.

"Why does Mother like him?" I asked.

"Maybe you should ask her."

"She won't talk about it to me. She just says he's nice to her, but he's not."

Granddaddy pulled to a slow stop at the intersection. He looked both ways and swung the car left toward the coast.

"Your mother's entitled to her privacy," he said. "And she knows how to take care of herself."

I saw he wasn't going to choose a side, so I dropped the subject and looked out the window. Even with a strong west wind the briny smell of seawater rarely drifted inland to Fourmile. The only reminder that we were close to beaches was an occasional lone seagull passing nonstop over the pine trees.

Granddaddy pulled off the highway before the beach house he'd been looking for. It was still there, but it wasn't like he remembered. It was more modern and groomed, with a carport built onto the side.

"I spent ten straight summers here," he said. "Some of my best memories with your mother and grandmother were made right there."

I studied his face while he stared at the house. I could almost see the memories flipping through his head.

"I tried to buy it when they stopped renting it."

"What happened?"

"I guess it wasn't for sale. I don't really know. But I remember feeling like something was getting jerked out from under me. It didn't seem right to have gotten to know a place like that and then have somebody take it away from you."

"You missed it?"

"Yeah, but you move on."

He put the car into gear and turned around in the road. On the way back we stopped at the hardware store and purchased ten gallons of white paint and loaded it into the trunk.

"How much do windshields *cost*?" I asked him.

He studied me for a second, then chuckled. "Not as much as education, Foster."

Granddaddy stayed for supper and talked with Mother about the houses she'd been looking at in the paper. After the meal I went out to the barn to feed Joe. When I returned, Mother was putting the dishes away and Granddaddy was standing in the living room.

"Want to walk me to my car?" he asked me.

"You going back tonight? It's kind of late."

"What else does an old man have to do?" He smiled. But he knew what I was thinking. I followed him outside and shut the front door behind me.

"I wish you'd stay," I said.

He put his hand on my head. "I'd like that, but I better get back and check on your grandmother."

I looked at the ground and nodded.

"We'll be seeing plenty of each other real soon."

"Yes, sir."

He pulled his hand away and patted me on the back. "Be good to your mother," he said.

"I will."

I agreed to work off the money by painting the fence. There was nearly a quarter mile of it in a square around the house, two-by-four timbers notched into six-inch cedar posts. I started on the section out by the blacktop, thinking that if I wasn't able to finish it all, at least I'd get the part people saw.

Despite how he acted when we went to his house, Dax didn't stay away. It was no time at all before he was leaning on the kitchen counter with Mother smiling and wearing her perfume again. I was happy to have a reason to get out of the house.

All day Saturday and Sunday for two weekends I lugged around a gallon-can of paint, a brush, and a feed bucket to sit on. I found myself looking forward to the work. Besides a way to avoid Dax, it was something different to occupy my mind. When Joe wasn't chasing killdeer, he napped in the broomsedge nearby. Cicadas buzzed like electricity and breezes fluttered the tops of the pecan trees. In the breath of the hot asphalt I dipped and swiped paint. As much as it seemed time stood still on the farm, summer wasn't the only thing making its way toward Fourmile. I was about to meet a stranger who would change everything.

6

The air was balmy and windy under a sky of rolling gray clouds. I was halfway down the front fence, sitting on my bucket, when I saw him coming up the road with his dog. I'd never seen a person walking this stretch of highway. Joe stood and trembled with an inside whine that meant he was either nervous, excited, or both.

"Easy, boy," I said to him.

I went back to painting, glancing up from time to time as they drew closer. After fifteen minutes I heard the man's feet crunching the loose gravel on the roadside. I set my brush on the rim of the paint bucket and grabbed Joe's collar.

The man wore a tall frame backpack like I'd seen on hitchhikers before. I guessed he was about Dax's age, but maybe younger. He was dressed in blue jeans and a white undershirt with a camo bandanna tied around his forehead so that his hair was covered. On his belt he wore a hunting knife. He was medium height and thin like Dax, but there was something a lot tighter and healthier about him. The way the straps of the pack pulled against his shirt made his chest and arm muscles stand out like smooth river stones.

He stopped and knelt at the side of the road, putting a hand on his dog's head. "See a friend, Kabo?" he asked.

The dog was black with a little white under its neck. It seemed to be a mix between a collie and a black Lab, a mutt like Joe. Kabo wagged his tail and approached. I stood and walked Joe closer until their noses were touching.

"What's your dog's name?" the stranger asked me.

"Joe," I said.

"Good-looking dog."

Joe wasn't a good-looking dog appearance-wise, but I knew what the stranger meant. I figured he could see in dogs what a farmer can see in cows and horses.

"He's real smart," I said.

We let them sniff and circle each other. After a moment I let loose of Joe's collar and looked back at the stranger. "Where you going?" I asked.

"Texas," he said.

"You going to walk the whole way?"

"I might. I'm doing pretty good so far."

"That's a long way."

The stranger bent down and unclipped Kabo's leash. The dog bolted away with Joe in pursuit.

"Yeah," the stranger continued. "It's a long way. I don't plan to rush it."

There was something interesting about the man. Something young and fresh and adventurous I hadn't been around in a while.

"I've never seen anyone walk past here before," I said.

"I like to use the back roads. It takes a little longer, but it's a lot more interesting."

I watched him studying my painting supplies.

"You paint all the way to here by yourself?" he asked.

"Yes, sir. This is my third weekend working on it."

"Just call me Gary." He smiled.

"Okay," I said. "I'm Foster."

Joe and Kabo had jumped through the fence and were chasing each other through the pasture.

"This your farm, Foster?" he asked me.

"Yeah, but we're going to move."

"What do you grow here?"

"We used to raise cows, but we sold them all."

"It's a nice place."

I didn't answer him.

"You mind if I use your hose to fill up my water bottle?"

I was glad that my meeting with Gary was going to last a little longer. "I don't mind," I said. "I'll show you where it is."

A strong, cool breeze came across the tops of the pecan trees and a long shadow crept over us. The sweet smell of an afternoon squall was in the air. Gary looked toward the west and saw the line of bruised-looking clouds approaching. "Better bring your paint in," he said. "Looks like we might get some rain."

I realized he was right and began gathering my supplies. Finally we started toward the driveway. I knew Mother wasn't going to like me bringing a stranger to the house, but lately I hadn't trusted her judgment any more than my own.

7

The dogs fell in beside us before we made it back to the house. I showed Gary where the hose was just to the left of the front door. He hefted his pack to the ground and pulled a canteen from a side pocket and began to fill it. Kabo rubbed against him and Gary glanced at him. "I know, boy," he said. "Just hold on."

Gary stood and recapped the canteen and left the water running. Kabo began to lap from the stream. Then I heard the front door open and turned to see Mother standing there with a look of concern. "Hello," she said, more like a question than a greeting.

"Hey, Mother. This is Gary."

"Hello, ma'am," he said. "Foster offered your water faucet to me. I don't mean to be any trouble."

Mother looked at the highway like she was still trying to figure out where the stranger had come from. Meanwhile Gary stepped past Kabo and shut off the water. "My dog and I are hiking across the South," he continued. "We haven't had anything but creeks to drink from since yesterday."

Mother started to say something but didn't. I could see she was nervous about Gary. "That's fine," she finally said. Then she noticed my paint supplies on the ground. "Foster, are you finished painting for the day?"

"It looks like it might rain," I said.

She looked at the sky and frowned. "Okay then. Why don't you come inside and wash up. Dax is on his way over here to watch the game."

"What game?" I asked.

"I don't know. But you need to clean that paint off of you."

"Why do I always have to clean up when he comes over? He doesn't care."

"I care. And don't argue with me."

I frowned and turned to Gary. "See you later," I said. "That's cool about walking to Texas."

He smiled. "Good luck with the fence, Foster. Nice to meet you, ma'am."

I went inside and Mother came behind me and shut the door. "Foster," she said.

"Ma'am?"

"You don't bring strangers up to the house like that. Especially with me alone in here."

"He's nice."

"You don't know anything about him."

Thunder rumbled in the distance and I looked out the window to see Gary and Kabo and Joe walking down the driveway.

"I can tell he's nice," I said. "Joe likes him."

"Just don't do it again."

"It's about to rain on them."

"That's not our problem."

"He could stay in the barn until it stops raining."

"Foster, I told you that I don't want strange men around here when I'm by myself. Now, this conversation is over."

"Dax'll be here. Just until it stops raining."

She stared at me. "Foster."

"Come on."

She looked up at the kitchen clock.

"He won't even come inside," I said.

She sighed and shook her head. "Okay, fine. He can sit in the barn until the storm passes. Then he gets on his way again."

I smiled and bolted out the door.

"You still have to get cleaned up!" she called after me.

By the time we got back to the barn, the sky had grown dark and it was sprinkling rain. Gary set his pack against one of the hay bales and worked his shoulders in a circle. There was tenseness about him, but it wasn't half-cocked like what I sensed in Dax. It was buried and controlled.

"Joe'll stay out here with you," I said.

Gary looked at the two dogs, side by side in the hay. "I think Joe was ready to hit the road with us today."

"He would have come back," I said.

Gary cracked a strange half smile at the edge of his mouth. "I know he would have."

He felt raindrops hit his face and looked up at the hole in the roof. He stepped aside and studied it. "Might want to put that project ahead of the fence," he said.

"Mother won't let me climb up there."

"Where's your father?"

"He's dead," I said bluntly.

Gary nodded to himself, creating a moment of distance, but no shock and no pity. I waited for him to say something more, but he didn't.

"Mother's boyfriend's coming over," I continued.

He didn't seem to hear me. He was backing up, studying the hole in the roof. "You got some sheet tin lying around?" he finally asked.

"Yes, sir. There's four pieces leaning against the back wall."

"Gary, remember?"

"Sorry."

"Got a hammer and some nails?"

I pointed to the back of the barn at the equipment room. "In that room. There's a ladder hanging outside too."

He looked at me. "Let's go get it before this rain starts coming down too hard."

"You don't have to do that."

He looked out the barn door toward the road. He did a lot of stopping and looking around. It was like there were two sides of him going on at all times, the side I was involved in, and something else I didn't know anything about.

"I know," he said. "Come on."

8

I slid the sections of sheet tin up the ladder, careful that the gusts of wind didn't get under them and peel them away. Gary grabbed them from his perch on the roof. I waited until he'd nailed the missing pieces in place, then held the ladder for him as he came back down. By then the rain was starting to hit hard.

"That ought to hold for a while," he said. "Let's get out of this."

I followed him back into the barn, where it was dry and warm and darker, and the rain hammered on the tin like something we'd rudely locked out. Gary went to his pack and opened it and got another T-shirt. He pulled his wet shirt off and wiped himself with it. His movements were quick and efficient and rehearsed. He was all muscle, but lean like a skinned rabbit. I'd never seen someone so strong close-up. Finally he turned and draped the old shirt over the pack. Across his back was a giant tattoo of a skull wearing a beret. I had a brief instant to study it before he swiped his new shirt on and faced me. He knew I'd seen it. He knew I wanted to ask him about it. But something in his expression told me he was sorry he'd shown it to me.

"Looks like you got a lot of little projects around here," he said.

"Yeah."

"How big is this place?"

"Not as big as most farms. Two hundred acres."

"Big enough to stay ahead of you."

"Yeah. Mother's trying to sell it."

He nodded. I stood there, wanting to say something, but not knowing what. I just wanted to hear him talk. Gary sat down and leaned against his pack. He made a clicking noise with his mouth and Kabo rose from his bed in the straw and came to lie next to him. Gary stroked the dog and watched it and seemed to be thinking of something long ago and far away.

"We can't afford to fix it all up," I said.

Gary continued to stroke the dog and I didn't know if he was listening to me or not. Suddenly Joe woofed deep in his throat and stood. I felt a bolt of panic race up my back as I remembered about Dax coming to watch some ball game. I eyed the leash hanging on the wall.

"Come here, boy," I said.

Joe took a step toward the house.

"Joe!" I said.

He woofed again. I moved toward him, but it was too late. He bolted out into the rain.

"No, Joe!" I yelled.

I ran after him. Before I got around the side of the house I heard shouting and then a yelp that turned my stomach. I rounded the corner to see Dax standing in the rain, holding a tire iron. Joe was limping across the yard.

"What'd you do!" I yelled.

Dax threw the tool into the back of his truck, where it landed with a clang. Then he turned to me. "I was ready for him that time," he said.

I ran after Joe and caught up to him just as he reached the shelter of the big pecan tree. He turned and crabbed sideways before me and lay down with his feet in the air, rolling his eyes to the whites. I collapsed beside him and rubbed his stomach.

"Dax?" I heard Mother say.

I looked at the house and saw her standing in the front doorway, looking confused. Dax was still in the rain watching me. Then I saw Gary, seemingly out of nothing, standing silent and still on the other side of Dax's truck.

"I warned him, Linda," Dax said. "That mutt needs to be put down."

"Did he bite you, Dax?"

Dax spit at the ground and turned to her. "He damn sure tried. Would have if I hadn't've cranked one over him."

Mother looked across the yard at me. "Foster, I thought we talked about this. You're supposed to put him on the leash."

"It's my fault, ma'am," Gary said.

Dax spun at the voice.

"I had him helping me in the barn," Gary continued.

"Where the hell'd you come from?" Dax said.

No one seemed to notice the rain anymore. Gary motioned his chin at the blacktop. "I was walking up the road and they said I could sit out the storm."

"Walkin' up the road?" Dax said.

Gary nodded.

Dax looked at Mother.

"Come out of the rain, Dax," she said. Then she looked at me. "Foster, is he okay?"

I didn't answer her. I turned back to Joe and gathered him in my arms and struggled up with him. Then I carried him around the opposite side of the house toward the barn.

I laid Joe on his side in the hay. He was breathing fast and stared past me at the rain, his stomach rising and falling and a blankness in his eyes like something with no spirit. Gary knelt beside him and ran his hands lightly over his ribs, stopping just behind his foreleg. "Might have broken this one," he said.

"What should I do?"

"Nothing," he said.

I stared at him.

"Animals don't feel pain like us," he continued.

"Will he die?"

Gary shook his head. "I don't think it's that bad. If he punctured a lung he'd have blood coming out his mouth."

"It doesn't hurt him?"

"Not in the way you think."

"He looks like he's hurt."

"His body knows to take it easy and rest. It's instinctive. I'd call it more confusion than pain."

"How do you know?"

"It happens to people too, but they have to be hurt a lot more than this. You go into shock and it overrides the pain."

"Foster!" I heard Mother calling. I looked up and saw her watching us through the rain.

I turned away and didn't answer.

"Is he okay, Foster?" she called.

Gary lifted his hand and nodded at her.

"Put him on the leash and come inside," she called.

"So he'll be better?" I asked Gary.

"He'll be better. I'll watch him for a while."

"I don't want to go inside."

"You need to do what your mother says."

I studied him. I couldn't believe he was taking her side too. But I'd do anything for him. I didn't know why, but I trusted him more than I'd trusted anyone in a long time.

9

Mother had made spaghetti for lunch. The pasta was steaming in a colander in the sink and a pot of sauce simmered on the stove. Dax stood shirtless in the kitchen wearing a pair of Daddy's old jeans and rubbing his hair with a towel. I felt him watching me as I passed.

"Sorry about your dog," he said.

I knew he didn't mean it. I ran into Mother as she came out of the living room. She pulled me to her and hugged me. I remained stiff and stared at the wall.

"I'm sorry, Foster," she said. "I told you to keep him tied."

I didn't answer her. She put her hand through my hair and I pulled away from her and went to my room to change.

I stared at my spaghetti. No one was saying anything. Dax had also put on one of Daddy's old T-shirts and it made me sick to see it. He ate like nothing had happened.

"What's with the guy in the barn, Linda?"

"Foster met him this morning," she said. "He just wanted to sit out the rain."

"You don't need to be lettin' strangers hang around like that."

"I knew you'd be here," she said. "He seemed nice enough."

"What's his name?"

Mother looked at me.

"Gary," I said.

"What is he, a hitchhiker?"

"He's walking to Texas," she said.

"He's a little off the track for Texas."

"He said he likes to take the long way," I said.

Dax studied me. "Maybe you ought to make some friends your own age."

"Dax," Mother said.

"What?"

"I've got the fence to paint," I said. "I don't have time for friends."

"Gonna take you two months to finish that thing. And I don't remember you havin' any friends before."

"That's enough, Dax!" Mother said.

Dax put down his fork and sat back in his chair and chewed. "Well, this is loads of fun, ain't it?"

Mother looked at her plate and didn't argue.

Dax pushed himself away from the table. "Look, I got some stuff I need to do this afternoon anyway."

"That might be best," she said.

He studied her for a second like he didn't like her answer. Then he took one last gulp of beer and stood. "Yeah," he said. "I'll call you later. Spaghetti was good."

She made a weak smile at him and let him go. When I heard the door shut behind him, I looked at her. "I don't like him wearing Daddy's clothes."

She dropped her fork and stared at me. "Foster, I'm trying hard. I'm trying really hard."

"He wants to kill Joe."

"He didn't want to kill him."

"He would have."

"He tried to bite him, Foster."

I looked down and didn't answer her. Neither of us ate or said anything for a minute.

"I can't replace your dad," she finally said. "Nobody can do that."

"Then don't try," I mumbled.

I heard her sniffle and knew she was crying. I felt sick about it, but there was nothing to take back. I wasn't sorry about anything I'd said.

I tried to think of something to make her feel better. I looked at her. "Gary fixed the barn roof," I said.

It took her a moment to remember who Gary was. Then

she wiped her eyes with her napkin and composed herself. "He did what?"

"He fixed the roof. I helped him."

She seemed surprised. "Well, that was nice of him."

There was a knock behind me. I suddenly realized the rain had stopped and turned to see Gary stepping back from the door and waiting patiently. At first, just the sight of him put me at ease. Then I realized he had probably come to say goodbye and my spirit sank.

"Get the door, Foster," Mother said.

Kabo stood beside Gary, and behind them I could just see Joe lying in the barn where I'd left him.

"I wanted to say thanks for letting me get out of the rain," he said. "Joe's going to be fine, Foster. Let him rest for a while. He may be a little slow for a few days, but he'll come around."

I nodded.

Mother came up behind me and put her arm around my chest. "I'm sorry about all the drama," she said to him.

"It's no problem, ma'am."

"Foster told me you fixed the barn roof."

"He helped me. Took us about five minutes."

"Thank you," she said. "It's been— That was nice of you to do that."

Gary studied her for a moment, reading something in her. "Ma'am," he said, "I realize—"

"Please don't call me ma'am. It's just Linda."

"Okay. I just wanted to throw this out. Foster told me you're trying to sell the place. It's a nice spread, but you could get a lot more for it if you did a few things to shore it up. I could use the work."

I turned and looked up at her, but she avoided my stare. She knew what I was thinking.

"I appreciate the offer," she said. "It's not possible for me right now."

"If it's the money you're worried about, I'll work for minimum wage. I don't need much."

Mother hesitated. "What sort of work can you do?"

"I used to work for a general contractor. Pretty much whatever. Engines and electrical too."

"Engines?" she said.

I looked back at Gary.

"You could get five thousand dollars for that farm truck if you got it running," he said.

"That's a lot of money," she said.

"Replace this roof and you could tack eight to ten thousand dollars on the value of the house. But I'd start with the things people see right off. Help Foster finish the fence, mow the pasture, haul off and sell the equipment you don't need."

Mother's hand slid off me. I turned to her and saw her finger her hair behind her ear and take a deep breath.

"It's going to take me forever to finish the fence by myself," I said.

She thought about it. "That sounds like a lot of work," she said. "How long do you think all that will take?"

"Three weeks. Maybe a month. I'll move on whenever you want."

"But—"

"I'll need a place to stay," he interrupted. "If you'll rent your barn to me I can pay you thirty dollars a week. And I won't charge you my labor to fix the truck if I can use it while I'm here."

Mother shook her head. "That's a very generous offer, but I'll need to check with Dax about it."

"Dax?" I said.

Mother looked at me for the first time. "Foster, you stay out of this."

"I understand," Gary replied.

There was an awkward moment while all of us stood there and no one said anything. "Foster, go check on Joe," she said at last. "And—I'm sorry, what was your name?"

"Gary."

"Gary, let me call Dax and see what he says about it."

I stepped out the door and stood beside him, swelling with hope.

"I'll be in the barn with Foster," Gary said.

When Mother came back out to the barn, she was carrying two blankets and a pillow. I couldn't contain my smile and looked up at Gary. He glanced at me and the hardness in his eyes went soft for just an instant.

She stood before us and held the bedding out to him. The look on her face told me she'd made up her mind about something. Once Mother decided on a thing, there was no arguing against it.

"Okay," she said. "I can't say I'm completely comfortable with the arrangement, but I need the help and that's all there is to it. Get the truck running and you can use it to pick up supplies and groceries and whatever else you need. You're responsible for your own meals. I don't want any drinking on the property and I don't want you bringing any friends over."

Gary nodded. "I don't expect you to cook for me. I don't drink and I don't know anyone to bring over."

"You know what I'm talking about."

"I know. There won't be any surprises."

She took a deep breath. "Good," she finally said. "Let's get this place cleaned up."

10

The clouds moved away that afternoon and the sun beat down on the farm. Gary said he thought we should start with the truck so that we'd be able to use it for runs into town. We left Joe and crossed the yard with Kabo following. We approached the covered shed where Daddy's old truck and tractor were parked. I'd not been so close to them since Granddaddy had parked them there a year ago. As we came near, I looked at the driver's-side window and an image of Daddy sitting there with his hand flopped over the steering wheel made me draw a sharp breath. Gary slowed and studied me for a moment, but I didn't look at him and kept walking.

He stopped just under the shed roof and turned to me. "When's the last time either of these things ran?"

"About a year ago."

"Is that when your dad died?"

I nodded. "He had an accident in the woods out back." *Please don't ask me anything more*, I thought.

"Key's in it?"

"It should be," I said. "Should be a key in both of them."

"Go stand by the hood while I pop it," he said.

I walked around to the front of the truck and waited while he stepped to the driver's door. It creaked open and an image of exactly what lay scattered across the bench seat flashed through my head. Three red 12-gauge shotgun shells, a copy of *Game & Fish* magazine, a crescent wrench, and a manual to our portable generator. On the passenger-side floor were two empty Sunkist soda cans. I knew what Gary smelled inside. Diesel and wet rubber. Suddenly I heard a clunk and saw the hood pop up about an inch. I took another deep breath and made myself step forward. I slipped my fingers under the lip of the hood and lifted it. Gary appeared beside me and studied the engine. "Let's check the fluids before we try to crank it. I doubt the battery's good anyway."

I knew how to do it myself but stood back while Gary checked the oil and transmission fluid. He seemed satisfied with both. After a quick inspection of the belts he walked back to the cab. "See how she feels," he said.

I heard the ignition buzzing as he turned the key, then the engine began to drag. Gary leaned over and turned off the heater and the engine suddenly roared to life, white exhaust pouring from the rear. He stared at the instrument panel as he pumped the gas pedal and raced the motor. After a second he let off and looked at me through the glass. "I'd say that's a pretty good start," he said.

I nodded.

He left it running and got out. "We'll let the battery charge for a few minutes."

"Okay," I said.

"The oil level's good, but we better change it. Pretty old."

I heard him, but I was looking through the windshield at the empty cab.

"You all right?" he asked me.

I turned to him. "I'm all right," I said.

His eyes studied me like he knew everything. "What do you say we look at the tractor while we're out here?" he said.

"Okay," I said.

We weren't as lucky with the tractor. I had to get the jumper cables from the barn and we hooked them to the truck and jumped it off. Once it cranked, a squealing sound came from beneath the cowling. I showed Gary where the spare belts were hanging on the barn wall and we replaced them and greased the fittings on the Bush Hog. When we were done he stood back and looked around.

"That fence is still too wet to paint," he said. "And I need to make a list of supplies before we go into town. What do you say we use what daylight we've got left to knock some of that grass down in the field? It's probably dry enough now."

"Okay," I said.

"You know how to drive this thing?"

I shook my head. "I've ridden on it before, but I never could reach the pedals."

"I imagine you're a lot taller than you were a year ago. What would your mother say about you learning?"

I felt a rush of excitement. "I don't know," I said.

"Go ask her."

I heard the tractor crank behind me as I barged into the kitchen, slamming the door against the stop. Mother wasn't there, so I dashed into the living room and almost knocked her down.

"What's wrong, Foster!" she said.

I caught my breath. "Gary wants to know if I can Bush Hog!"

She looked over my shoulder and out the kitchen window. "Certainly not," she said.

"He said he'd teach me!"

She put her hands on her hips. "Foster, the answer is no. That's a dangerous piece of equipment."

"Who's going to cut the grass when he's gone?"

"I don't plan on being here long enough to worry about that. I just called the real estate agent and told him to lower the price again. I don't care if we have to take a loss to get on with things."

I knew she wouldn't budge. She had her jaw set with that same look of resolve I'd seen earlier. I sighed and turned to go.

I sat on the back fence and watched Gary driving the tractor from one end of the north pasture to the other, shaving perfect slices of cleanly cut field grass. The sun sat low in the sky, just over the far trees, and a buzzard circled high overhead. Something about the vision—about the sense of progress—loosed the knots inside me. It had been a long time since I'd felt the health of a blue sky and the pasture and the smells of the cut grass and insects. Then I turned and looked to the east, to the wall of trees that hid the creek bottom and the back sixty acres. I hadn't meant to look, but maybe I had. Maybe I wanted to see if this new feeling was strong enough to overcome the sight of that dark place. But it wasn't. A vision of what I'd seen that day flashed into my head, hot and searing. I jerked my eyes to Gary again and swallowed, but my chest was already tight and my throat dry. I took a deep breath and trained my eyes on Gary, watching him like you watch the horizon to make seasickness go away. I watched him and fought the memories and lied to myself about the man I saw on the tractor. I ran the lies through my head, over and over again, until I'd run off the nightmares.

11

I sat in the barn that evening with Joe and Kabo lying on either side of me. We watched Gary prepare his new living arrangements. Joe was still acting sluggish and sore so I rubbed his neck to let him know I was thinking about him. Gary had left his wet clothes from earlier in the day to dry in the sun and he changed shirts again, this time facing me so that I couldn't see the tattoo.

"Where'd you find him?" he asked me.

He was talking about Joe. Maybe he guessed I'd not raised him from a puppy, but something told me it was just something else he knew. "He came out of the creek bottom. I don't know how old he is. I've had him since I was eight."

Gary studied him. "I'd say he was about ten years old."

"How do you know?"

"I checked his teeth earlier. And he's got a little gray around his mouth."

I looked at Joe's mouth. "How long do you think he'll live?" I asked.

Gary didn't answer me right away. He stepped over to his pack and put away his Dopp kit. Then he dug around and pulled out a length of thin rope and began to tie it to one of the support columns. "He looks like he's got plenty of life left in him," he finally said.

He walked the rope to another column and tied it like a clothesline. Then he draped his sweaty shirt over the middle.

"What will we do tomorrow?" I asked.

He came back to us and sat and leaned against his pack. "I figure it'll take me two days to mow the rest of that pasture."

"What can I do?"

"Why don't you keep painting the fence? I'll come join you after I'm finished with the field."

I looked away and frowned. I could feel him watching me.

"Or we can both work on the fence tomorrow. I can finish mowing while you're in school."

"Let's do that," I said.

"Okay," he said with his crooked smile. "You're the boss."

I smiled and nodded.

It was hard to keep my mind on supper with Gary out in the barn. Mother kept glancing at me across the table. I didn't know what she was thinking. I didn't want to ask her anything because I was afraid she'd say no to it.

"Dax told me not to let him stay," she said.

I looked at my glass of water and didn't respond.

"But Dax doesn't have my problems," she continued. "We can't keep living like this. I've got to do what I can to get us out of here."

I couldn't imagine her disagreeing with Dax. I looked up at her. "What'd you tell him?"

"I didn't tell him anything. It's not his decision."

"Gary's good at fixing stuff," I said. "He can do anything."

She scooted her chair back and stood. "Gary's all we've got right now," she said. "Go fix a plate for him and take it out there. Tell him I know he hasn't had time to get groceries."

I felt my spirit surge again. I gulped down my water and stood.

"Foster?" she said.

I looked at her. "Ma'am?"

"Give him the plate and come back."

When I stepped into the barn, Gary and Kabo weren't there. I heard the faucet running out back and Joe rose from his bed in the straw and came to me. I knelt and ran my hand along his back.

"Doing okay, boy?" I said to him.

Joe shuddered with excitement and rubbed against me. I looked over his back and saw the clothesline. Gary's pants and the bandanna he wore on his head were now hanging on it. On the ground were his things, pulled from the pack and arranged neatly on a dark blue blanket. Several cans of food, a first-aid kit, three books, a bound sheaf of folders, separate stacks of pants, shirts, underwear, and a spare set of black high-top boots. But what interested me most was a large automatic pistol. I stood and walked closer and studied it. Daddy had a pistol, but it was a smaller-caliber revolver. He carried it under the truck seat to use on snakes. Now Mother kept it inside the house.

"Looks like Joe's feeling a little better," I heard.

I turned to see Gary standing in the opening at the opposite end of the barn with Kabo next to him. He rubbed his head with a towel, shirtless and barefoot with blue jeans on. When he pulled the towel away I saw the top of his head for the first time. Black hair close-shaved to within a quarter inch of his head.

"I brought supper," I said, holding out the plate.

He walked to the clothesline and used both hands to neatly drape the towel over it. I got another glimpse of the sinister tattoo on his back.

"Mother said you haven't had time to get groceries," I said.

He glanced at his belongings on the blanket then turned to me. "Tell her thank you for me. Set it on top of those hay bales over there."

"It's meat loaf."

"I see. It looks good."

I put the plate down while Gary pulled on a T-shirt. Then he knelt on the blue blanket and began putting his things back into the pack. There was a certain order to everything. The folders first, then the stacks of clothes.

"What kind of pistol is it?" I asked.

"M9 Beretta," he replied.

"Daddy had a pistol."

He kept packing and didn't answer me.

"Daddy's was for snakes."

"Is this going to make your mother nervous?"

I shook my head. "She doesn't mind guns."

"She might mind somebody else's . . . I usually keep it packed out of sight."

"I won't tell her about it."

Gary didn't answer me. He put two of the three books away and finally only the pistol and a rag were left. He picked up the handgun and dropped the clip and swiped back the action seemingly in one quick motion, like he'd done it a thousand times before. Then he took the rag and stood and stepped over to the wall where one of our old grease guns hung. He drew his finger across the tip of the grease gun and scraped the lubricant onto the barrel of the pistol. He came back to me, rubbing the handgun with the rag.

"Have you ever shot a snake?" I asked.

"No," he said. "But I've eaten one."

"Really?"

He glanced at me and smiled. "Yeah. Doesn't taste bad. All reptiles taste pretty much the same."

"I had frog legs once," I said.

"Then you know what a snake tastes like."

"What kind was it?"

He picked up the clip and wiped it and shoved it back into the grip. "I don't know," he said, snapping the chamber closed. He wrapped the rag around it and placed it into the pack. Then he reached over and scratched Kabo behind the ears and looked at me. "You want me to feed Joe?"

I realized I'd forgotten. It wasn't like me to forget things like that. "I can do it," I said. I turned and started for his bag of food I kept in a metal trash container against the wall. Joe followed behind me.

"I don't want to hurt your mother's feelings, but Kabo and I already ate. You can give him what's on that plate if you want."

"No," I said. "He eats special dog food. It's expensive."

"I see."

"It helps with his tricks. He can do a lot of tricks."

"Like what?"

"He can fetch and climb ladders."

"Climb ladders?"

"Yeah. He could've gotten on that roof with you today."

"No kidding?"

"Serious," I said.

I scooped out some of the dry food and dumped it into Joe's bowl at my feet. He lowered his head to it and began eating.

"How'd you teach him to climb ladders?"

"When I first found him, he'd try to do just about anything I wanted. One time I went up into a pecan tree to get the pecans and I saw him trying to come after me. He figured out how to stand on the rungs and pull himself up with his front legs. He's real smart."

"Dogs have big hearts," he said.

I came back to Gary. He was sitting on his blanket, leaning against the pack with his hands behind his head. His face and eyes seemed free of the tension and alertness he'd been carrying all day.

"He can catch armadillos too," I said. "He'll pin them to the ground and hold them there until I tell him to get off."

"How'd you teach him that?"

"I didn't. He just started doing it for me because I thought it was funny the first time."

Gary nodded, thinking to himself.

"I better get inside," I said.

"Yeah. You going to be ready to go in the morning?"

"I'll be ready."

He picked up the book and put it in his lap. I tried to read the cover but couldn't see it well enough. "Good night, Foster," he said.

"Good night."

12

I rose at daybreak, dressed, and went out into the damp morning to see if Gary was ready to work. The sun was just coming over the trees at the far edge of the pasture and a hawk soared overhead. Small birds and squirrels chattered in a way that told me it was going to be clear and sunny.

I walked into the barn and found Gary and the dogs gone. The clothesline was empty and his blanket was neatly folded and draped over the top of his pack. I heard a banging sound past the barn and kept walking until I saw them in the pasture. Gary was leaning over the back of the tractor and Kabo was darting across the field. Joe lay near the fence, his head up, watching me.

"Hey, boy," I said.

He got up and trotted to me and sidled against my leg.

When we reached the tractor Gary stood, shoved a socket driver in his pocket, and wiped his hands on his pants. "Loose UV joint," he said.

"You get up pretty early," I said.

He looked past the house and toward the blacktop. "I don't need as much sleep as I used to," he said.

"I used to get up early. But sometimes there's not anything to do."

He looked down at me. "You ought to find plenty to do on a day like this. A boy your age."

"There's nobody around to play with."

He started toward the barn and I fell in beside him.

"Do you ever have friends over?" he asked.

"I used to."

"What happened?"

I didn't answer him right away. "We're moving," I said. "I don't want any friends from here."

"But you had some before?"

"Yeah."

"What about *them*?"

"I don't know," I said.

"Yes you do."

"I got in a fight with one of them."

"Over what?"

"I don't know."

"Yes you do."

"He was bragging."

"About what?"

"His dad."

"You were jealous," he said.

I didn't answer. I felt a pang of shame course through me. We came to the fence and I crawled through and Gary stepped over. We continued on.

"That's okay," he said. "But you should get right with him."

"I know," I said, relieved that he wasn't upset with me.

"You shouldn't leave that kind of thing behind. It's hard to imagine, but it all comes back to you one day."

It was strange the way he talked to me. Like he was talking to me and someone else at the same time. Maybe himself. But I thought about what he said, even though I didn't fully comprehend it. I didn't mind him lecturing me, if that was what he was doing. I wanted to know what he thought about everything. I could tell he knew about a lot of things. He was the first person I'd felt like talking to since Daddy died. And there was a lot I wanted to ask him, but I couldn't do it. Not yet.

We had just finished getting the painting supplies ready when Mother called me in to breakfast.

"Go on," Gary said. "We need to wait a little bit for the sun to dry off this dew."

For some reason Mother was in a good mood. She leaned against the counter and watched me hurry through a breakfast of bacon and eggs and toast. It had been a while since we'd had anything but cereal. After I was done she fixed Gary another plate and sent me out with it.

This time Gary took the plate and ate standing up. The dogs and I watched him and waited patiently until he had scraped the last of it clean. Then he gave the plate back to me and picked up the gallon of paint in one hand and the empty bucket with our supplies in the other.

"Run this back inside and tell her it was the best I've had in weeks. Then grab another bucket to sit on and meet me out front."

13

The blacktop was still cool and wet and empty. Cicadas buzzed in the weeds of the ditch and a flock of crows made steady noise from the pecan orchard. Gary was already painting as I made my way down the fence with my bucket. Joe trotted up beside me and I reached down and stroked him behind his ears. I glanced at Gary and saw him watching us.

"I think he's better now," I called to him. "Watch this."

I set down my supplies and picked up a stick. I placed the stick on top of a fence post and Joe eyed it and whined.

"Hold," I said to him.

Joe trembled as I stepped back.

"Get it!" I said.

Joe whimpered and looked at me with shame.

"Usually he'll jump up and grab it," I said.

"Don't push him," Gary replied. "Give him a little more time."

I took the stick from the post and held it out to him. Joe took it in his mouth and I gave him a reassuring pat on the back.

Once I got to work, the two dogs settled into the grass next to each other and began to soak up the morning sun. Gary knelt on the inside of the fence, facing the road, and I stood on the outside. We dipped our brushes and started wiping on the paint. By the time we'd finished one section and repositioned our bucket seats for another, we'd found our rhythm. Since Gary was faster he brushed his side as well as the underside and top of each rail. We kept the paint next to me since his arms were longer. These things were done without words and the work filled me with a sense of accomplishment I'd not felt in a long time.

"Where'd you grow up?" I asked him.

He kept painting and didn't look at me. "Lots of places," he said. "My dad was in the military. We moved around."

"Where's your family now?"

"My mom's in Maryland. Dad's in Virginia."

"Do you ever call them?"

"It's been a while."

"How come?"

He stopped painting and dipped his brush into the bucket again. "I don't know," he finally said. "I've been meaning to."

"Do you like being by yourself all the time?"

"I've got Kabo to keep me company."

"Where'd you get him?"

We heard a car coming and Gary stopped his brush and looked up. He watched the car as it approached and didn't look away until it passed. Then he dipped his brush again.

"I had a summer when I didn't do much. Just before I went into the army. I got him from the kennel when he was a puppy."

"Then you left?"

"That's right."

"I'll bet he was glad to see you again."

"Yeah. I thought maybe he wouldn't recognize me."

"But he did."

Gary nodded and smiled. "Like I hadn't been gone more than a day."

"Does he know tricks?"

"Not much. He's mostly just a friend."

"I could teach him some."

"What for?"

The question surprised me and I wasn't sure how to answer it. "Just so he'd know some," I said.

"You think he wants to know tricks?"

"I don't know."

Gary stopped painting. I could tell it was time to move the buckets. We picked them up and scooted down again. I thought I might have upset him and I was uneasy about it.

"Sometimes I wonder if Kabo wants to be on the road with me. The asphalt's hard on his feet. Meals aren't always regular. People can be selfish when it comes to dogs."

"You think it was wrong to teach Joe tricks?"

Gary looked at me and seemed to realize what I was feeling. "No," he said. "I didn't mean that. I was sort of thinking out loud. I guess I just meant that I've already asked a lot of Kabo."

I started painting again and breathed deep as a wave of relief passed over me.

"Kabo's really all I've got left," Gary said. "He's my family now."

The questions that hung in my head were ones I didn't have the courage to ask. I said nothing.

"I don't think I'll ask more than that of him," he said.

14

That evening Mother called me in to clean up and get my clothes out for school the next day. I said goodbye to Gary and the dogs and trudged toward the house. We'd painted almost the entire south section of fence. My back ached and my muscles were sore, but all of it in a way that felt good and healthy.

I was standing in the shower with my eyes closed, letting the warm water run over my face, when I heard a car horn. I opened my eyes and listened. Then I heard Joe barking and a bolt of panic shot through me. I swiped off the water, jumped out of the shower, and threw a towel around myself. The horn continued to blow, mixed with Joe's frantic barking. By the time I got to the living room Mother was opening the front door.

"Linda!" I heard Dax yell.

She swung the door open and the headlights of Dax's truck were on our faces. Joe was standing outside the driver's door, snarling with the hair on his back standing up.

Dax shut off his headlights. After a second he leaned out the window. "Get this *damn* dog out of my face," he said. I could tell he'd been drinking by the way his head swayed and his jaw hung slack after the words.

"Joe!" I heard Gary call from the corner of the house.

Joe took a step back, not wanting to leave.

Gary made the clicking sound with his mouth and Joe woofed and crabbed around the front of the truck, keeping his eyes on it the entire time.

"You didn't tell me you were coming, Dax," Mother said.

Dax watched Gary grab Joe by the collar and didn't answer.

"I tried to catch him," Gary said. "I'll go tie him up."

"Thank you," Mother said.

Gary walked around the house, pulling Joe beside him. Dax got out of the truck and faced Mother. "So I got to make reservations now? I got to call ahead so you can put the mutt on a leash?"

"He doesn't usually act like that, Dax. We're not used to having to keep him tied up."

"Well, if I got to call ahead every time I wanna come by, we're gonna have to make some other arrangements."

"Just come inside, Dax."

He didn't move. "What's that guy still doin' here?"

"Come inside, Dax."

"Don't dodge my question, Linda. What the hell's he still doin' here?"

"I've hired him to help fix the place up."

"I thought we talked about that. You don't know anything about him."

Mother didn't respond.

"Do I have to ask you again?"

"No, Dax. I answered your question already."

"You tryin' to get into it with me? I've had a long day, sweetheart. I ain't up for it."

"Dax," Mother said wearily. "I'm not trying to start anything. I told you I hired him because I need the help. He's staying out in the barn."

"For how long?"

"I don't know."

Dax started to say something else but didn't. "Where'd you get the money to hire somebody?" he finally said.

"None of your business," I said.

He looked over at me. "What'd you say?"

"Foster, get inside!" Mother said.

I didn't move and I didn't take my eyes off him. "I said it's none of your business. We need the help."

Dax took a step toward me. "I'll throw you over the hood of this truck and remind you what it's like to have a daddy whip your ass."

"Dax! I think you need to leave."

He stared at me for a moment, then swung his eyes back to Mother. "You know, I came over here to apologize for the way things went down yesterday, but I can't even get in your front door now without gettin' dealt a bunch of crap."

"I'll call you tomorrow, Dax."

He turned and started back for his truck. He took a couple of steps, then faced Mother again. "Don't start actin' like we're married, Linda. That's when it stops for me."

He watched her like he expected an answer, but she didn't respond. Finally, he turned and got into his truck. He cranked it and peeled out backward, swung it around in the yard, and tore across the gravel. Mother grabbed my shoulder and steered me inside. As I turned I caught a glimpse of a dark form beneath the big pecan tree. Something out of place. Gary standing quietly in the darkness, watching everything.

15

G o to your room," she said. "I taught you better manners than that."

"I can't keep him tied up all the time."

"Foster, if he bites Dax we're going to have to put him down."

I felt anger boiling up into my throat.

"It's a liability that I can't afford," she continued. "Now go on."

I didn't move. "I told you before that I hated him. And I won't ever like him."

She stared at me.

"Never," I said.

The next morning I dressed for school and ate a quick breakfast of cereal. Through my window I saw Gary mowing far across the pasture. Mother and I didn't say a word to each other until it was time to leave. Then I went and got into the car and waited for her. After a moment she came out of the house in her postal uniform and locked the front door and got into the driver's seat.

"You never used to lock the door," I said.

"Give me a break, will you, Foster?"

I looked at my lap and didn't say anything as we pulled out onto the blacktop. We drove along in silence until we got to the fourway where the school bus picked me up. Mother shut off the car and rolled down her window. I heard birds chirping and the sound of another tractor rumbling away over a field to our left.

"I've got some concerns about Dax too," she said.

I didn't respond, but I was surprised to hear it.

"But that doesn't give you an excuse to act like you did toward him."

"I can't help it," I said.

She turned to me. "Foster, at least make me feel like I'm doing okay at this by myself. At least give me that."

"It'd be a lot easier if Dax was gone. It was fine before he came around."

"No, it wasn't fine. But I'm not saying he's made things any easier."

I didn't have anything to say.

"And surely you've thought about how a dog like Joe's going to move to Montgomery with us."

I looked at her. "What do you mean?"

"He can't just roam around there like he does here. He'll have to stay penned up."

"I know."

"Maybe he ought to start getting used to it."

It was something I'd thought about but kept putting out of my head. Joe had been a free roamer all his life. It was hard to imagine him penned up anywhere. But it was even harder to imagine life without him.

"Foster?"

"Ma'am?"

"It's going to be a change for the better, but all of it won't be easy."

"I know," I said again. But I didn't. I just wanted her to stop talking about it.

I used to like school, but now I hated it. It seemed useless to like it anymore since I'd be leaving it and everything I'd known to move away and never see the places and people again. I quit the baseball team after Daddy died. I just stopped going to practice and Mother wasn't in any shape to notice. When she finally did ask about it, I told her I didn't want to do it anymore and she didn't argue with me. He used to come watch. I couldn't bear the thought of being on the field and looking in the stands and not seeing him there. Everybody was moving on while I was stopped. School was only a place I went to and came back from. I was glad I only had a week left before summer break. But Gary's words about making things right with my old friend hung in my head, and I had to do it because he'd told me to and he was the only person who knew about anything. Even if I didn't fully understand what he told me, I knew I could do it without having to think about it and it would be the right thing just because he'd said it was.

I approached Carter on the playground during recess. He stood under the cedar tree where we used to sit and scratch tic-tac-toe in the dirt. He had his back to me, talking to some other boys.

"Hey, Carter," I said to him.

He turned and looked at me.

"I'm sorry about the fight," I said.

He nodded. I could tell it was awkward for him. Something he didn't expect and didn't have words for. The other boys were watching and listening.

"I like your dad," I said. "I got jealous."

He swallowed. "I thought you were moving," he said.

"I am. We're still trying to sell the house."

I knew he wouldn't tell me to join them. I was too far outside their circle now. But I didn't expect or want him to.

"Okay," he said. The pressure of the other boys watching us was pulling him away from me. But I'd done it. And something *did* ease inside me, even if I didn't give the feeling any value.

16

ary finished mowing the pasture and continued painting the fence while I was at school. In the afternoons I
hurried home, ate a quick dinner, and went out to help him
as the sun dropped over the pasture trees and the frogs
cheeped in the roadside ditch. The wet, hot air of summer
grew heavier each day as spring trailed behind us. Even
the rattling of the cicadas was sluggish and the air smelled
of wilted lettuce.

Gary went into town and supplied himself with food, a
box fan, and a few new items of clothing. There was an old
refrigerator in the shop that Daddy had used to store beer
in the bottom and wild game in the freezer on top. We
cleaned it out and plugged it in so that he would have a place
to keep sandwich meat and milk and other things that
would spoil.

In the evenings I sat in the barn with the moths darting about the single bulb overhead and the fan blowing gently over us. The smell of the freshly mown pasture was so strong and thick it seemed you could chew it. The humming of the refrigerator condenser was something I hadn't realized I'd missed. It brought the barn back to life in a way that I remembered too well. But as long as Gary was with me, I wasn't afraid.

He didn't seem to mind me watching him. I held my questions until he finished feeding himself and Kabo. Then he washed his face and changed his shirt. Finally, he sat in his usual place, leaning against the pack like it was something to protect. He would sharpen his hunting knife or clean his fingernails or repair a tear in his clothes with a small sewing kit. Quiet, simple things. And I finally let my thoughts fall carefully in that air of subtle tension that hung about him.

"Where'd you get the tattoo?"

He didn't answer me right away. He was using a hand towel to dry a metal cup I'd seen him drink and eat soup from. It reminded me of the way the priest had cleaned the chalice when we'd gone to church.

"Where? Or what does it mean?" he said.

"What does it mean?"

"Special Forces."

"What's that?"

"It's part of the army . . . I got it in Iraq."

I looked back at the stick I was whittling and shaved off

another slice of bark. I was using a hunting knife Daddy gave me for my tenth birthday. I'd brought it out to the barn hoping that Gary would ask me about it, but so far he hadn't seemed to notice. Now I wasn't thinking about the knife and only moving it as something for my hands to do while the questions raced in my head.

"Have you killed people?" I asked the ground.

When he didn't answer I glanced up just in time to see him nod. But he wasn't looking at me. He was agreeing to something bigger and my question was only a small part of what he was answering.

"With that pistol?" I asked.

He placed the cup he was cleaning back into the pack and turned to me. "No," he said. "Not with that pistol."

I didn't have the courage to ask him more. The way he studied me. There was something about him on the edge of somewhere, like a coiled spring that would release if I made the wrong move, said the wrong thing. I saw it in his breathing, in the muscles beneath his shirt. It was a frightening sensation that I'd never experienced. But I knew it had nothing to do with me. I knew that I was completely safe—safer than I'd ever been in my life. What I was frightened of I didn't know.

"I saw you under the pecan tree," I said. "When Dax was here."

"I know you did," he said.

"You would have beat him up."

"It's not my place to get in your mother's business."

"But you would have."

"He'd had a lot to drink."

"But that's why you were there, wasn't it? You would have beat him up?"

He looked at Kabo and rubbed his hand over the dog's neck. "I would've stopped him if he'd taken things too far."

I looked down at the stick I'd stopped whittling and took a deep breath and smiled to myself without meaning to.

"Foster," he said.

I looked back at him and tried to get rid of the smile.

"I want you to be careful around him."

I felt the smile go away.

"I don't care what you think about him, don't ever smart off to him again."

I nodded.

"You understand?"

"Okay," I said.

"Your mother's a smart woman. Things with her boyfriend will work out."

"I told her I didn't like him."

"And she heard you. I promise you that."

17

When I came in the back door, Mother was standing in the kitchen. The lights were off and I couldn't figure out what she was doing there in the darkness.

"I don't want you getting too attached to him, Foster," she said.

"What do you mean?"

She thought for a moment. "I mean like you are about Joe."

"I've just been helping him."

"I've seen you out there. And a mother can tell certain things."

"What's wrong with him?"

"Grown men don't decide to walk across the country unless they're leaving some problems behind."

"You mean he did something bad?"

"I mean he's going to be gone soon and I don't want you upset over it."

"I just like to talk to him," I said.

"I know it's been a while since we've had a man take an interest in this place, but don't forget that he's only doing it for the money. Then he's gone. Like we never knew him."

I didn't like what she was telling me, but I had no argument against it.

"So don't get too attached to him," she said again.

"I'm not," I said.

I didn't hear Mother talk about Dax that week and I wasn't going to ask her about him. By Friday evening Gary had finished the south end of the front fence and moved on to the shorter north end. He said that with my help the next day he thought we could finish. Then we'd go into town and get supplies for re-roofing the house.

Saturday morning I met Gary in the barn after a quick breakfast of cereal. We had some time to kill until the dew burned off, so I helped him fix two fence rails that had come loose. Then we gathered our paint supplies and hauled them out to the road. Joe and Kabo raced across the field and I was happy to see my dog acting like his old self again.

"How do you like being out of school?" Gary asked me.

"Good."

"It'll be nice to have some full-time help."

I smiled to myself and hefted my load a little higher.

We set our buckets where Gary had left off the day before and got to work.

"When we move to Montgomery, he'll have to stay in a pen," I said. "You think he'll hate it?"

"He'll be fine as long as you're with him," Gary said.

"I don't know what I'd do if he couldn't come," I said.

Gary kept painting and didn't answer.

"I thought we'd always be here," I said. "I didn't think we'd ever leave."

"There's not much in life you can hold real tight to, Foster. I'm sure you've got a lot of good memories here. You'll make some more in another place."

His words triggered a white-hot flash of images from that day in the creek bottom. It came across me so suddenly that I made a strange noise from deep in my throat. Gary stopped painting and studied me for a second.

"Everything all right?" he asked.

I nodded and started moving my brush again, trying to suppress my thoughts. I could sense his eyes still on me.

"You want to tell me about it?"

"No," I said suddenly. It had never seemed possible that I could talk about it with anyone.

I heard his brush swishing again. "I didn't say that like I wanted to," he finally said. "I lost my dad too."

I didn't answer him. I didn't want to say or think about anything until I was sure the images were gone.

"Not in the same way, but the end result was no different."

I looked at him again. "What do you mean?"

"I let him down."

"How?"

"It doesn't matter. But I have good memories. It wasn't anything he did."

I didn't reply.

"Let's move on down," he said.

We worked silently for a while as the sun rose over the pasture and the shadows receded into the far trees.

"What do you like to do, Foster?" he asked.

"Like what?"

"That's what I'm asking you."

"I used to play baseball," I said.

"But you quit?"

I nodded. He glanced at me and continued painting.

"I like *this*," I said.

"Painting?"

"Yeah," I said. "Working on the farm. I wouldn't just do it for Dax."

We heard the trucks approaching just after noon. As usual, Gary stopped what he was doing and grew tense and alert. He watched them through the shimmering vapor of the blacktop until they were close enough for me to recognize Dax's truck. I felt my stomach turn.

"It's Dax," I said.

"I know," Gary replied. "Remember what I told you."

18

Dax slowed and stopped in the road before us. The other truck, a green Dodge dually with HADLEY TRENCHING on the door, stopped behind him pulling a large flatbed trailer. Mounted on the front of the truck was a black iron grille guard and a Warn winch. The pickup's oversized knobby mud tires, chrome roll bar, and guttural, throbbing muffler were enough to tell me everything I needed to know about the two men inside. But I'd seen them before. They'd dropped Dax off at the house once. They were big and dirty and didn't have anything to say to me or Mother.

Dax rolled his window down and looked us over. "You might get to the end of this thing yet," he said with his friendly voice.

I glanced at Gary. I could tell he was studying the second truck. Then his eyes swung back to Dax.

"How you doin', Foster?" Dax said to me.

"Okay."

Then he looked at Gary. "I'm Dax," he said. "Met you the other night."

Gary nodded at him.

Dax motioned to his friends behind him. "Linda said that tractor was for sale. I brought my buddies by to pick it up. She said you got it runnin'."

"It's a good tractor," Gary said.

"We got a deer camp we could use it at to plant green fields."

"There's a disk behind the back fence. I'm sure she'd sell that to you as well."

"Really?" Dax said.

Gary nodded. "That and the Bush Hog hooked up to it."

Dax smiled and winked at him. "I figured the implements came with it."

Gary didn't smile. "That's about a thousand dollars' worth of equipment you just threw into the deal."

The smile left Dax's face. "Well, I'll talk to the owner about that."

Gary didn't reply. Dax looked across the pasture at Joe. He looked at me again. "I'm gonna get your momma some cash in her pocket, kid. That oughta make her happy."

I didn't respond. He smirked and looked back at Gary. I

felt the tension between them like a rope stretched taut between their eyes.

"I don't think I like the way you look at a fellow, mister."

Gary didn't answer him.

Dax finally turned away and started rolling up the window. "Make sure that dog stays out of my way, kid," he said.

The trucks pulled off and we watched them turn in to the driveway.

"She should have asked me about it," Gary mumbled.

"The tractor?"

"All of it," he said.

Dax's friends left with the tractor, Bush Hog, and disk chained to the flatbed. Gary didn't look up from painting, but I watched them until they were out of sight. Then I looked back at the house and a sick feeling crawled over me when I saw Dax's truck still there.

"He didn't leave," I said.

"I know," Gary replied. "Keep painting and get your mind off it."

Late that afternoon we came to the end of the fence. Gary finished his part and waited until I'd brushed my last strokes. Then he stood and backed away and stared down the long line we'd painted over the last two weeks.

"Proud of it?" he asked.

I stood and turned over my bucket and dropped my brush into it. I looked down the fence and I *was* proud to see what we'd done together. Then my eyes wandered over to Dax's truck.

"Come on," Gary said. "Let's wrap up."

Joe and Kabo were far across the pasture, chasing something. I picked up my bucket and walked with Gary to the barn. I took my time putting the supplies away in the equipment room while he stood next to me rubbing paint off his hands with a rag and gasoline. When he was done he tossed the rag to me and I caught it and wiped my arm and fingers. He leaned against the workbench and watched me until I was done.

"I'll come see you after supper," I said. "Will you tie up Joe for me?"

He came away from the counter and I followed him out of the equipment room. He sat down against his pack and put his hands behind his head. "Have a seat," he said. "Why don't we hang out until she calls you."

I was happy to stay. I couldn't help smiling to myself as I sat across from him.

"Let me see your knife," he said.

I dug into my pocket and pulled out the Barlow and passed it to him. He opened the blade and studied it and scraped the pad of his thumb across the edge. Then he leaned forward and turned to get something out of his pack. He reached deep inside and dug about until he had what he was looking for. His hand came back with a rectangular leather case with a necklace of dog tags tangled around it.

"Is that what you wore around your neck in the army?"
I asked.

He untangled the ball chain from the case and tossed it to me. "Yeah," he said. "Sometimes. Depended on what we were doing."

I studied one of the metal tabs.

```
CONWAY
GARY L
423-27-9646
O POS
EPISCOPAL
```

"Your last name's Conway."

"Yeah."

"What's the number?"

"It's my social security number. Right under that's my blood type. O positive. Then my religion."

"Why do they need to know the religion?"

"In case I got killed. They'd know how to bury me."

The tags felt warm in my hands. Gary opened the leather case and pulled out a whetstone. He spit on it and rubbed my knife blade in a flat, circular motion. "You want them?" he said without looking up.

I nodded. He continued working the blade. "They're yours," he said.

19

It was past our usual suppertime when Mother appeared at the back door. She called me and I came out of the barn so that she could see me. She looked tired and guilty and the spirit I'd seen in her lately was gone. I heard Dax's truck start and drive away.

"Foster, come inside," she called.

I shoved the dog tags in my pocket and turned back to tell Gary I'd see him later, but he had come up behind me. "I'll walk over there with you," he said.

Mother waited for us. "I'm so sorry, Foster. I just lost track of time."

"It's okay," I said. "We finished the fence."

She started to turn like she might be able to see it, then realized her mistake and faced us again. "That's wonderful, Foster."

"You mind if I have a word with you, Linda?" Gary said.

She looked at him with a little surprise. "No," she finally said. "Come inside."

We all started for the back door.

"It'll just take a minute," he said.

I stood in the kitchen with the two of them, waiting to hear what he had to say.

"Foster, go to your room and wash up," she told me.

I frowned and turned to go. I walked into my room and stood in the center of the floor and listened.

"I don't want to overstep my bounds," he said, "but I can help you out when it comes to what some of the farm equipment's worth."

"I just want it gone," she said. "I'm past trying to get a good deal."

"I understand. But I might be able to get a better price for you real quick at the feed store. They have advertisements posted on a bulletin board."

"Dax said he priced the tractor for me. Maybe I'll need your help when it comes to the truck."

There was a pause. "Okay," he said. "Just let me know. It won't hurt to have a number in your head for some of these things."

"Thank you, Gary. Is there anything you need out there?"

"I'm fine, thanks. Tell Foster I've got some errands I need to run tonight. I'll feed Joe for him and see him first thing in the morning. We'll need to start stripping the shingles off the roof early before the heat hits us."

There was another pause.

"Gary," she said.

"Yeah?"

"Be careful with him," she said.

"I know, Linda," he replied.

She heated some leftover spaghetti for me and placed it on the table with a glass of milk. She didn't fix anything for herself, but sat across from me and watched me eat. I stared at my plate and picked at my food. I didn't want to talk to her.

"Gary said he's got some things he needs to do tonight," she said. "He wants you to help him with the roof in the morning."

I kept eating and didn't answer.

"What's wrong?" she said.

I didn't look at her. "You know what's wrong."

"We really need the money."

"You could have sold it to somebody else."

"It seemed like the best thing to do."

I looked at her. "I thought he wasn't coming back."

"He wanted to apologize, Foster."

"Gary doesn't like him either."

She sighed and got up from her chair. "I can't talk about this tonight," she said.

"Me neither."

I lay in bed that night, staring at the dog tags on the bedside table and holding my closed pocketknife in my fist. My head raced with too many thoughts for sleep to come. Eventually I heard the farm truck crank. I got out of bed and stepped to my window and looked out in time to see him pull around the house toward the blacktop.

Sunday morning we started at daybreak. Gary got on the roof of the house, scraped the old shingles up with a flathead shovel, and flung them off. I busied myself on the ground, picking up the pieces and tossing them into the farm truck.

Mother brought us bacon and eggs and biscuits after we'd been at it for an hour. Gary came off the roof and we stuffed them down and got back to work within a few minutes. The cicadas were already rattling with the oncoming heat.

By ten o'clock Gary had his shirt off and glistened with sweat. The smell of hot tar and pine hung thick in the air while his shovel scratched and popped across the loose grit and plywood. His back muscles rose and fell against it all as he tore it away. Occasionally he'd stop and take the bandanna off his head and wipe his face with it.

For the first time I was able to study the tattoo as much as I wanted. It was a haunting image that spoke only of death. I couldn't help but think it had to be connected to whatever it was Gary thought about when he grew distant with me.

"Hammer," he called down to me.

I got the hammer out of the truck and tossed it up to him. He caught it and smirked like he was impressed.

"That's too good an arm to waste," he said.

"It was just an underhand toss," I said. But I knew what he meant.

He knelt and began using the hammer claw to pull up some stubborn roofing nails. I caught them as they rolled off the edge and tossed them into the truck bed with the other trash.

Just before noon he came down the ladder and leaned against the truck. He took off the bandanna and wiped his face again and draped it over the side rail.

"Must be a hundred ten degrees up there," he said.

"You need some more water?"

He glanced out at the blacktop then looked at me. "Yep. A lot of it. You got a swimming hole around here?"

"There's Tillman's bridge about five miles up the road. You can swim there."

He pushed himself away from the truck. "Sounds good. Go get your swimsuit on. Ask your mother if she wants to go. Lunch is on me."

"Mother?"

"That's right. I'm going to get a dry shirt and shorts out of the barn. I'll meet you out here in ten."

20

I knew Mother would be surprised about Gary's invitation, but I never thought she'd accept it.

"I don't think I'll swim," she said, "but I could get out of this house for a spell."

She changed into a wide-brimmed straw hat and a sundress I hadn't seen in a long time. Then she moved about the house gathering her sunglasses, three beach towels, and a John Grisham paperback. She held that same resolute expression I'd seen when she decided to hire Gary.

We loaded the dogs into the farm truck and set out with the windows down, me sitting between the two of them. Gary pulled onto the blacktop and shifted through the gears, and the sound of the truck, the feel of the acceleration through the seat and the tires on the highway and the faint popping of the muffler were all familiar, things pulled from a dark closet. Gary smelled like tar and sweat, but in a good way. Mother held her hat in her lap and her hair swished about her face in the breeze. The heat brought a healthy flush to her cheeks. As muggy and hot as it was, a deep sense of contentment coursed through me and gave me chills. This time, I let my imagination have its way.

The creek ran tea-colored over polished gravel and white sand. Bay trees and water oaks grew tall from the bank and shaded all but a sunlight-dappled area in the center. The effect was that of a cool tunnel with sparrows and thrushes calling from deep in the tangled walls. The dogs leaped in and waded in circles. After a moment they both turned and looked at us as if to tell us it was okay.

"We're coming," I said.

Satisfied, Joe lowered his head and started lapping up the cool water. Kabo headed upstream toward the dark shade of the bridge.

Mother sat on a towel a few feet back from the bank and laid her book open beside her. Gary and I stepped to the creek edge and contemplated the water.

"It's cold," I said.

He stripped off his shirt and hung it on a branch. The tattoo was in full view. I glanced at Mother and she averted her eyes and placed a hand on her book. Gary waded into the shallows and fell backward and sat up on his elbows. He looked at me and grinned. "Man up, kid," he said. "It's worth it."

I hung my shirt beside his, backed up, and tackled the

water. I fell into the shallows, the water so cold it burned. I rolled over and sat up and crossed my hands over my chest and gasped. Joe splashed up to me and began licking my face until I shooed him away. He didn't seem to mind and crashed off upstream after Kabo.

The creek licked my ribs and I felt the heat in my cheeks fade. My body slowly relaxed and I eased back onto my elbows into the coolness.

"You're missing out," Gary called up to Mother.

She smiled and finally picked up her book.

"There's bass in here," I said to him. "If you walk down-stream a little ways you can find some deep holes. They hang out in the cut banks."

"You ever caught any?"

"It's pretty hard in this clear water, but I used to catch some."

Gary stood and looked downstream. "Come on," he said. "I'll show you a trick."

I got up and waded after him, the cool-off giving me new energy. It was only a second before the dogs caught on to our plan and came splashing after us.

"Where are you two going?" Mother called.

"Fishing," Gary said. "We'll be back in a minute."

Mother set her book down again and watched us until we were out of sight.

I knelt in the shallows, holding both dogs by the collar. Gary lay flat on the creek bank just downstream from us.

He had one hand in the water and the other was at rest beside him. Kabo whined and trembled with anxiety.

"Shhh," I said. "It's okay."

Minutes passed while Gary remained as still as a log. Nothing about him even twitched except for his eyes, which blinked occasionally. The dogs grew impatient and tugged at their collars, but I held them and waited. Eventually I saw the hand in the water ease along the bank a tiny bit. A few more seconds passed. Then his other hand inched away from its resting place and stopped just above the surface. Suddenly he plunged it into the water and his arms jiggled about.

"You got one!" I yelled, leaping up. Kabo barked and lunged forward, pulling me face-first into the creek. I let the dogs go and struggled to my feet again. When I stood Gary was in the water, lifting a two-pound bass from the shallows. The dogs crashed up to him and circled him, eyeing the fish.

"How'd you do that!"

He turned to me and smiled. "Practice."

I started toward him. "Can you show me?"

He knelt with the fish and cradled it into the water again.

"Wait!" I said. "We can eat it."

He paused and looked at me. "Kind of small, don't you think?"

"No, we can eat it. I want to eat it."

He shrugged and lifted the fish back out of the water

and tossed it onto the bank. "You better catch another one if you want to make a meal for us."

"Show me," I said.

We lay side by side just as Gary had been earlier. It wasn't much use with the dogs pacing before us and scaring the fish, but Gary said he'd tell me what to do and then he'd hold Joe and Kabo while I tried.

"You make your finger look like a worm," he said. And I saw his hand below the surface and his pointer finger slowly curling and uncurling.

"Keep it moving real slow. When the fish gets close, start tickling his belly."

I looked at him and laughed. Gary remained focused on his finger.

"It works," he said. "It sort of relaxes them. You'll notice when they get calm."

I studied his finger again, moving in the clear depths.

"Then you ease your other hand over," he said, sliding his left hand off the bank and slowly positioning it over the imaginary fish. "Get it below the surface so you don't splash. Stay a little behind him."

I watched as the top of his hand sank into the water.

"Then snap!" he said, bringing both hands together. He withdrew his arms and flicked them dry and turned to me. "Think you can do it?"

I didn't think so, but I nodded anyway.

We moved downstream and Gary held the dogs while

I tried his technique. I could see the bass, suspended in the dark water beneath the overhanging tree limbs, but couldn't attract them to my fake worm. After five minutes my finger was so cold that I couldn't bend it, but I didn't pull it out. I didn't want to give up. I wanted him to see me catch one.

"Maybe we'll try some more after lunch," he said. "My stomach's starting to growl."

I was relieved to have an excuse. I sat up and saw the bass dart away. "I think I was close," I said. "They were looking at me."

"It takes a while to get the hang of it. Let's head back and eat."

21

I carried the bass back with us and showed it to Mother and told her how Gary had caught it with his hands. She acted impressed.

"We're going to eat it for supper tonight," I said.

"You need to keep it cool," she said.

Gary started for the truck. "Let me get lunch out of the cooler and we'll put the fish in it."

He brought back a small Playmate lunch cooler that I remembered seeing in the equipment room, where it was filled with nails. He came over to Mother and knelt and took three sandwiches, three bags of potato chips, a thermos, and three paper cups from it. He placed them all on the towel and motioned at me with his chin. I brought the fish over. The inside of the cooler was scrubbed clean and a Ziploc bag of ice cubes lay across the bottom. I placed the fish inside and he closed it.

"I hope everybody likes ham and cheese," he said.

Mother smiled and reached for a sandwich. "I didn't know your kitchen was so stocked," she said.

Gary opened the thermos and began filling three cups with water. "Best accommodations I've had in a while," he said.

Mother got the other two towels out of the beach bag and we spread them side by side. I sat in the middle and we faced the creek and ate our lunch while the dogs lay in the shade under the bridge. Gary chewed slowly and seemed to be catching up on his thoughts of that other place he carried in his head. Mother glanced at me occasionally, but mostly stared over the water. I could tell she wasn't completely comfortable and maybe not seeing the creek at all, but not sure where to look or what to say.

After a few minutes Gary got up and took the cooler back to the truck. He stayed there for a moment, kneeling beside Kabo and scratching behind the dog's ears. When he came back he dropped a plastic grocery bag in my lap. "For the trash," he said.

Mother wiped her mouth with the corner of her towel. "That was good, Gary."

"I never had a bad picnic," he said. "Foster, let's clean up and see if we can get some more fish."

I watched him catch two more bass that afternoon. I

tried a few more times myself, but despite his encouragement, I wasn't able to get the fish to approach me. By the time we started back upstream the creek was darkening with the shadows of late afternoon. The bird calls were less and more shrill in the breezeless air and the thrumming of the cicadas had faded. Squirrels fussed from the treetops, waiting for us to move on so they could come down and feed. I walked beside him, the dogs trailing us, finally too worn out to care about dashing ahead. My skin felt tight and sunburned on my face.

Mother packed the towels while Gary and I put our shirts and shoes back on.

"That's an interesting tattoo," she said.

Gary pulled his shirt on. "Yeah," he said. "I guess sometimes you get caught up in the moment of things."

"Must have been quite a moment."

Gary looked at her. She smiled and looked away.

He started for the truck. "I was young," he said.

"You're still young," she replied.

We loaded the dogs and then Gary opened the truck door for me and I swept by and climbed in. He followed and leaned over me and opened Mother's door. She said "Thank you" and got in beside me. Gary popped the bandanna out the window to get the sand off and tied it around his head.

"And that?" she said.

He looked at her. "I'll bet I get more use out of this rag than anything else I own."

"You don't seem the type to be into fashion."

He grinned and started the truck and pulled out from under the bridge. "I don't want you to take it the wrong way, Linda, but whether you're into it or not, I think *you* look real nice today."

I stared straight ahead, not wanting to look at either one of them.

"Thank you," she said again.

I couldn't help glancing at her. She looked out the window and smiled to herself. She hadn't taken it wrong at all.

The sun was setting and the air coming through the truck was cool on my sunburned skin. The sound of crickets played from the forest at the edge of the road and the smell of pine sap and dust flowed into my nose. I felt like I could have ridden that way forever, between the two of them.

"We got a little behind today, Foster," Gary said. "We'll finish stripping the roof in the morning and head into town to get the shingles before lunch."

Mother turned to me. "You know I have to work tomorrow," she said. "You think you'll be okay by yourself?"

"I'll be okay," I blurted out.

"I'll keep him busy," Gary said. "He won't have time for mischief."

It was the best day I'd had in a year. Every bit of it down to the sunburn and the sand in my damp shorts. And the thought of spending the days ahead with Gary made my heart swell.

But the feeling didn't last long. The house came into view and the sight of Dax's truck parked in our yard yanked it from my chest.

22

When we turned in to the driveway Dax was coming around the side of the house. He saw the truck and all of us in it and stopped and stared. I could tell he was upset.

"Great," Mother said wearily.

We were halfway up the drive when Joe started growling from the truck bed and Gary stopped and got out.

"Get Joe and take him around back," he told me.

I slid across the seat and dropped to the ground. "Tell him to leave, Gary," I said.

"Just do what I told you. I'll meet you back there."

I frowned and walked around the truck. I dropped the tailgate and got Joe by the collar and pulled him out. "Easy, boy," I said.

Gary climbed back into the truck and started it toward the house. I tugged on Joe's collar and got him moving after them.

Gary pulled the truck sideways before the front door and parked it and looked out the window at Dax. I was angling around the house but close enough to hear them.

"Where the hell you been?" Dax said.

"You talking to me?" Gary said.

Dax craned his head to see past him into the cab. "No, I ain't talkin' to you," he said. "I'm talkin' to her."

"Then you talk nice to her."

I stopped and squeezed Joe's collar tight in my fist.

Dax straightened and looked at Gary again. "What'd you just say to me?"

Mother got out of the truck in a hurry. "It's okay, Gary," she said. She started walking around the hood with Dax's eyes on her the whole time.

"What is this, Linda?" he said.

She fingered her hair over her ear and I could see her hands shaking. "It's nothing, Dax. Gary and Foster wanted to go cool off at Tillman's bridge and I rode with them."

"Since when have you done anything like that?"

She stopped and looked him in the eyes for the first time. "Come on, Dax. We just went for a ride."

"I get here and your car's in the driveway and nobody's around. What the hell you expect me to think? Been lookin' all over the place for you."

"I told you to call first, Dax," she said.

"Call first! I'm supposed to be your damn boyfriend! I got to call to come check on you?"

She said it softly, but I heard it. "You're not my boyfriend, Dax."

Dax started to say something but didn't. He glanced at Gary then back at Mother. "I see," he finally said. "This is what you do when old Dax ain't around."

Gary opened his door and got out and stood there with one hand holding the window frame.

Dax turned and faced him. "Partner, I'm about to step over there and accept your invitation."

"You want him to leave, Linda?" Gary said.

Mother looked at the ground and nodded.

Dax stared at her in disbelief. After a second he began chuckling and shaking his head. Finally he spit at the ground. "I'll be damned, Linda. The hired help. I never—"

Gary took a step toward him. "Get in your truck."

The smile left Dax's face as he looked at Gary again. "Yeah, bud," he said. "Me and you'll talk again when the woman and kid aren't around."

Gary didn't answer him.

"You sure this is what you want, Linda? Don't be callin' me up tomorrow."

"Get in your truck," Gary said again.

Dax smiled and backed away, watching Gary. Finally he looked at Mother one last time before turning and getting into the S10. He cranked it and tore out of the driveway.

"You all right?" Gary asked her.

She nodded to herself and hurried into the house. Gary turned to me and motioned to the barn with his chin.

Gary heated two cans of soup for us and we sat in the hay with the dogs and ate out of paper cups.

"You think he'll come back?" I asked.

"Yeah."

"How do you know?"

"I know the type."

"But you'll beat him up?"

"I hope I can just talk to him."

"But you could beat him up. I know you could. You could, couldn't you?"

"Maybe."

"Why'd she ever like him?"

"You can't always tell about a person right away."

"But you knew. You knew the first time you saw him."

Gary lifted another spoonful of soup and didn't respond.

"How'd you know?" I asked.

"Your dog told me."

I looked at Joe. Gary reached over and petted him and Joe's ears twitched and I heard him sigh. "They have a sense we don't have," he said. "They can tell about a person. I don't know what it is."

"Joe growled the first time he saw him."

Gary didn't answer.

"You think I should go inside?" I asked.

He dipped his spoon into the soup again. "In a little while," he said. "Let your mother have some time to herself."

"What about the fish?"

"I'll clean them later and put them in the refrigerator."

"Maybe for tomorrow night?"

"Yeah," he said. "Maybe so."

"I had a good day," I said. "The best time in a long time."

He was distant again. "Good," he said.

"Gary?"

He wasn't looking at me. "Yeah?"

I knew what I wanted to ask. I had the words for it this time, but as soon as they built in my throat fear made me swallow them away. I didn't think I could take the answer. He finally looked at me.

"What?" he said.

I turned away and shook my head like it no longer mattered. He kept his eyes on me and I felt that he'd come back to me from wherever he'd been in his mind.

"I had a good time too," he said.

23

When I stepped into the house it was dark and quiet. I passed through the kitchen and down the hall and stopped before Mother's bedroom door. I listened for a moment and heard nothing. Then I knocked and she told me to come in.

She was lying in bed reading the book she'd taken to the creek that afternoon. I expected her hair to be unkempt and her eyes to be red from crying, but she was composed and you never would have known anything unusual had happened. She placed the book in her lap and raised her eyebrows at me.

"Good night," I said.

"Good night, Foster."

I started to go, then turned back. "Gary says Dax'll come back."

"Then I'll tell him to leave again."

"You said he wasn't your boyfriend."

"That's right. I don't want to see him anymore."

I breathed deep and smiled to myself.

"I didn't use good judgment, Foster. I'm sorry."

"It's okay," I said.

"Did you eat?"

I nodded. "Gary had some soup."

"What else did he say?"

"He said you can't always tell about a person right away. He said Joe knew Dax was mean the first time he saw him."

Mother looked down at her book, but she didn't pick it up.

"Gary could beat him up," I said.

She looked at me again. "Did he say that?"

"No. But I know he could. He was in the army. He's the strongest person I've ever seen. He's not scared of anything."

She started to say something but didn't. "I know you're having fun working with Gary, but I told your grandfather we'd come to Montgomery on Friday and spend the weekend. I want you to look at the school you'll be going to. I also have a meeting with a real estate agent to look at houses."

It surprised me to feel a rush of panic. Just a few weeks before I would have given anything to get off the farm and go see Granddaddy. But now all I wanted was to stay at Fourmile and work with Gary.

"But we haven't even sold the house yet," I said.

"I know. But I've got a good sense about things and we need to keep moving forward. And your granddad has a surprise for you."

"What is it?"

"A surprise."

"We'll be back Sunday?"

"That's right. And there'll be work left to do."

"Like what?"

"The barn needs to be cleaned out. There's a lot of touch-up painting to do inside the house."

"What else?"

"We'll see. That's plenty for now."

"But what if the house doesn't sell?"

"Foster, we're not staying here through the fall. I don't care if we have to sleep on Granddaddy's floor."

I looked down and nodded.

"So we both need to prepare for that."

"I know," I said. But I didn't really know at all.

The next day we finished taking off the old shingles and hauled our truckload of debris to the county landfill. Before heading into town for more supplies we stopped at a gas station and fueled up the truck and bought hamburgers and Cokes from a snack shop next door. We took our lunch with us and Gary pulled off the road at a public boat launch on the river and we ate on the tailgate.

"What's on your mind?" he asked me.

"Nothing."

He took another bite. "Okay," he said.

"I gotta go to Montgomery this weekend."

"Your mother told me."

I looked at him. "When?"

"This morning while you were out playing with Joe."

"But I'll be back Sunday."

"I'm not going anywhere."

"You could stop working and wait for me to get back."

Gary smiled. "I think I can manage for a couple of days."

"I don't want you to finish."

He looked out across the parking lot.

I didn't take my eyes off him. "There's still a lot to do, isn't there?" I said.

"I'll keep working as long as your mother needs me," he said.

"We could paint the rest of the fence. That would take a while, wouldn't it?"

He nodded. "That would take a while."

"I don't want to go to Montgomery."

He looked at me. "You need to go, Foster. I told your mother I thought it was a good idea."

"Why?"

"Remember when I said I thought that Dax would come back?"

"Yeah."

"I don't think you need to be around until he's had some time to cool off. This is a good weekend for the two of you to get out of town. There's things you need to do anyway."

I felt better, knowing my weekend away helped solve the Dax problem.

That evening Mother and I played checkers at the dining room table. It seemed neither of us could concentrate. It was hard not to glance at the kitchen window and wonder what he was doing. After a while we heard the truck crank and saw the headlights swing across the yard. We both watched until he was gone.

"Where do you think he goes at night?" I asked her.

Mother looked at the checkerboard again. "Maybe he goes to the store."

"It doesn't seem like he buys much."

"Maybe he doesn't need much."

I studied the board. "I'm kind of tired of checkers," I said.

She sighed and stood. "Me too. Let's finish another night."

"Mother?"

She turned back to me. "Yes?"

"Do you ever feel like Dad's here?"

A concerned look came over her. "I don't know what you mean, Foster."

"Sometimes I think I should be able to feel him. I've tried to, but I don't."

She shook her head like she wanted to say something but couldn't think of the words.

"I don't see how somebody can just go away like that."

"He's always with us in spirit, Foster."

"But that's just something people say. I don't know what it means."

"It means he's thinking about us."

"But I think he would want to tell me some things. Like he'd find a way."

"Like what things, Foster?"

I shook my head. "I don't know. Anything."

"Some things you just have to believe, even though they're hard to imagine."

I nodded.

24

Tuesday morning, I found Gary under the equipment shed, pouring oil in the truck. I held out a biscuit Mother had wrapped in aluminum foil. He set the oil on the ground, straightened up, and took it.

"Sausage biscuit," I said.

He leaned against the support timber and began to unwrap it. Joe trotted over and rubbed against my leg and I reached down and scratched him behind the ears.

"Check the dipstick," he said.

I walked to the truck and pulled the stick. I wiped the tip with a rag and slid it back into the tube. I pulled the stick again and noted the oil in the FULL zone. "Looks good," I said.

"Why don't you take it across the field?"

I turned to him. He was chewing, watching me. "Drive it?" I asked.

He nodded.

I glanced at the house.

"I already asked her about it," he said. "She's okay."

"She is?"

He nodded again.

"When?"

"What's it matter, when? Get in there."

I couldn't help but smile as I climbed into the driver's seat. My mind raced, trying to remember the sequence of events as I'd seen Daddy work them; depress the clutch, shift into first gear, turn the key to start it . . . But he had to be kidding me.

"By myself?" I asked.

"You know the gears?"

"Like an H. First is toward me and down."

"That's right."

"Seriously?"

Gary smiled. "Just start the damn thing. Then get out of here before she changes her mind."

I worked the column shifter into first gear, straightened my leg out against the clutch, and turned the key. The truck rumbled to life and Joe woofed at me. "I'm all right," I said down to him.

I gripped the steering wheel tight, let out the clutch, and bounced across the lawn with Joe in pursuit. I started to panic when the wheel was harder to turn than I'd imagined. I finally wrenched it around and headed for the pasture gate. Once I was going straight, I shifted into second and found the steering to be much easier. I swung to the left and headed for the north tree line, Joe racing along beside me.

When I arrived at the far trees I turned the truck and saw Gary coming across the pasture. I looked to either side of him but didn't see Kabo. He waved at me and held his hand up as a signal to stop and wait for him. I shoved in the clutch, studied the gearshift, and eased it into neutral. I let it idle until he came closer and swiped his finger across his throat. I reached down and turned off the key and studied him.

"What?" I asked.

"Let's take a walk."

I slid off the seat and dropped to the ground. "I did pretty good, didn't I?"

"You did *real* good," he said.

He walked around the truck and started for the thin strip of cottonwoods that separated the north end of our pasture from the neighbors. As he passed I saw the pistol stuffed into the back of his pants. I hurried after him.

"What'd you bring the pistol for?"

"Target practice. Grab Joe and keep hold of him."

"Where's Kabo?"

"I put him up. He doesn't like guns."

"What does he do?"

"He barks a lot. Gets unpredictable."

I grabbed Joe's collar and walked him next to me.

"Your dad ever teach you to shoot his pistol?" Gary asked over his shoulder.

"No, but I went hunting with him. I've used a shotgun. You gonna let me shoot it?"

"You want to?"

"Heck yeah!" I said.

We arrived at the edge of the woods and stopped. Gary looked around until his eyes rested on a tree about a hundred feet in the distance. Then he scanned the ground until he saw a plastic Coke bottle lying in the grass.

"Wait here," he said.

I waited with Joe while Gary took the Coke bottle to the tree. He jabbed a limb into the mouth of the bottle so that it hung in the air horizontally. On his way back he removed the pistol from his pants and snapped and clicked it with a few quick motions. He came to me and held it out. It looked big and heavy compared to Dad's revolver. I hesitated to take it.

"It's on safety," he said. "Go ahead and take it. Keep it pointed at the ground. Always keep it pointed at the ground, no matter what. Pistol's a lot more dangerous than a shotgun or a rifle."

"I know," I said.

He reached down and grabbed Joe's collar. "Good," he said.

I let go of Joe and took the pistol. It felt heavy and powerful and made me nervous.

Gary walked around behind me. "Grab it with both hands," he said. "Straight out in front of you. Let's see how you hold it."

I held it out and gripped it like I'd seen on television.

"Close," he said. He reached over my shoulder and adjusted my left hand and backed away. "Can you see down the sights?"

I lowered my face and peered at the Coke bottle through the metal sights. I nodded.

"Grip it tight, understand?"

I nodded again.

"Take it off safety," he said.

I clicked off the safety and looked down the sights again.

"Hold your breath, steady the barrel, and squeeze the trigger."

I took a deep breath, but I was too nervous to hold the barrel steady. I desperately wanted to get it over with. I closed my eyes and jerked the trigger. The pistol leaped in my hands and the concussion momentarily stunned me. I blinked my eyes and let out my breath, my ears ringing and the Coke bottle hanging motionless in the sunbeams. I felt a throbbing pain on my thumb.

"You jerked," he said. "Try again."

I took my hand away from the pistol and looked at my thumb. Blood was running down and dripping off my thumbnail. Gary noticed it and reached over my shoulder and took the firearm.

"The action hit you," he said. "You had your hand too far up."

I was getting queasy.

"You okay, Foster?"

My vision was blurring. I nodded. Then I felt his hand on my shoulder. "Sit down against this tree," he said.

I sat and leaned against a cottonwood tree, cradling my hand in my lap. Joe stepped up to me and licked my face.

"I should have noticed that," Gary said, kneeling beside me. "Suck on it. It's not deep."

I sucked on the knuckle and spit the blood into the leaves.

"It'll probably bruise a little," he said.

The knuckle throbbed and burned, but my dizziness was gone and the queasiness was ebbing.

"*You* shoot it," I said.

Gary chuckled. "I guess you've had enough for today."

I nodded.

"Well, don't be scared of it. I did that same thing the first time I shot an automatic."

"I'm not scared of it," I lied.

"You sure you don't want to try again?"

"Maybe tomorrow."

Gary stood and eyed the Coke bottle. "Watch what I do," he said. "Stand behind me."

He lifted the pistol in a smooth, mechanical motion and brought it to a dead stop straight out in front of him.

"Take a breath," he said, " . . . and squeeze."

Even though I was expecting the explosion, I jumped. The Coke bottle shivered on the branch just as the glint of a copper cartridge flashed and tapped into the leaves. Gary and the pistol remained still as a statue.

"You hit it," I said.

He didn't answer me.

"Shoot it again," I said. "Shoot it fast."

But he didn't seem to hear me.

"Gar—"

Suddenly the pistol was booming. The Coke bottle was straining like something tattered by a strong wind, bits and flecks of it spitting through the air. I slammed my hands to my ears.

He lowered the pistol and stared after the bottle, breathing heavy.

I was impressed and frightened and confused. "I think you got it every time," I said.

He ran his hand over the pistol in a quick motion, snapping the action shut, already swinging it behind him and cramming it into the back of his pants. He kept his eyes on the shredded bottle like it might move, like he'd be ready for it if it did.

"That was fast," I said softly.

He turned to me and studied me and nodded slowly. "Yeah," he said.

"What's wrong?" I said.

He was looking through me. "Nothing," he said.

I grew uncomfortable and didn't know what to say to him. My knuckle wasn't hurting anymore.

"I just wanted to show you how to shoot a pistol," he finally said, like he was making an excuse for something.

"Okay," I said.

He walked past me. "We'll try again another day," he said. "When your hand's better."

"What do I tell Mother about my thumb?" I asked.

"Why wouldn't you tell her the truth?"

"I don't know. I thought maybe—"

"Tell her the truth."

25

Before dinner Mother helped me clean the cut on my thumb. I told her about the shooting lesson and I was surprised when she seemed pleased about it.

"But I'm not that good yet," I said. "Gary's gonna let me try again when my thumb's better."

"That was nice of him to do that."

"He's the best shot I've ever seen," I said. "He can hit the target every time."

"He's probably had a lot of practice," she said.

"Can I have Dad's pistol?"

"Someday you can. Not any time soon."

I frowned. She pressed and smoothed the ends of the Band-Aid with finality. Then she put her hand on my head and looked at me. "But I'm glad you're interested in something again, Foster. It's nice to see that."

Before the week was out I drove the truck a few times during lunch while Gary sat on the fence and watched. We repaired a few rotten places on the roof and covered it with new felt and shingles.

Thursday evening I visited with him for a little while.

"Will you wait until next week before you go to the landfill?" I asked him.

"Never known somebody to like a landfill so much," he said.

"Will you wait for me?"

He smiled. "Sure."

"What about Joe?"

"Don't worry, I'll feed him."

"I'll shoot the pistol again when I get back."

"Okay."

"I know how to shoot a shotgun too, you know?"

Gary smiled again. "You told me."

"There's lots of things I know how to do," I said. "I just haven't done them yet."

"I don't doubt that," he said. "You better get inside and pack."

Early on Friday, Mother and I left the pastures and pine forests of Baldwin County behind. The country road turned to four lanes and the traffic gradually increased and we went with the flow of it onto I-65 north. In almost three hours we were in Montgomery, winding our way into the suburbs. Granddaddy's house was a small brick home in an older section of town. He'd lived there with my grandmother as long as I could remember and it seemed to fit them: modest and neat, nothing flashy, always there, always the same. As much as I couldn't imagine finding any entertainment there, it comforted me to know that there was one place I could go where nothing changed.

When we pulled into their driveway they came down the front steps to greet us. Grandmother was feeling better again, but I saw that she was moving slower and Granddaddy stayed at her side. I hugged her and shook Granddaddy's hand, something that still seemed a little awkward and funny to me. Then we all went inside and I waited patiently to find out what my surprise was.

Mother finally left for her appointment with the real estate agent and Granddaddy turned to me and gave me a teasing look. "Well?" he said.

I smiled and shrugged my shoulders like I had no idea what he was talking about.

"Want to see it?"

"See what?"

He turned and started for the back door. "Come on," he said. "I've got it out back."

It was a bicycle. A BMX bike like I'd seen some of the boys with at school. For some reason owning one had never occurred to me. It seemed so inferior to trucks and tractors and farm tools—so tied to sidewalks and city life. I'd learned to ride one when I was six, just before we left the city, and had been on them at friends' houses since. But I'd never thought of having one for myself.

I had mixed emotions about it. I saw the look in Grand-daddy's eyes, and I didn't want to hurt his feelings. But it seemed like taking it was agreeing to something I wasn't ready for. Not yet.

"I like it," I said.

"Take it for a spin."

I hesitated, then approached it and put one hand on the seat. "Where do I go?"

"Wherever you want. A boy needs his own set of wheels. Needs his freedom."

I got on. "I'll ride it on the sidewalk."

"Go up to the park. It's two blocks. Just make sure you look both ways when you cross the street."

"What about Mother? We were going to see the school."

"She might be a while. I'll tell her where to find you if she needs you."

26

The bicycle was light and smooth and the new tires hummed on the sidewalk. It was hard not to feel proud as I passed the houses, but I wasn't ready to admit liking any of it.

I heard the sound of children shouting before I saw the park. It consisted of a playground bustling with younger kids and their parents. Beyond it was a baseball field. A group of boys my age was assembled around the pitcher's mound in a loose arrangement that seemed either the beginning or the end of a game. I kept pedaling until I came to the fence behind the plate and stopped.

"Hey!" a short, blond-headed kid yelled. "You wanna play?"

At first I wasn't sure he was talking to me. It never crossed my mind that these strangers would be so casual with an invitation. I didn't answer right away. Then I realized the kid hadn't taken his eyes off me. His hair was so blond it was almost white.

I automatically shook my head.

"We need one more," he said. "We got a glove and bats."

"I don't know how long I can stay," I said.

"Come on," he insisted. "We got to have one more."

I was still trying to find an excuse while I got off the bicycle. I knew they were going to embarrass me. But they were all looking at me now, and as impossible as it seemed, I wanted to play.

The boy detected my indecision and started toward me. I leaned the bicycle against the fence and walked around to meet him.

"I'm Cory," he said. "What's your name?"

"Foster."

"Come on," he said. "We aren't that good or anything."

Something about him put me at ease. He turned and I followed him toward the group.

"I like your bike," he said over his shoulder.

"Thanks."

"Where you go to school?"

"I'm not from here," I said. "I mean, I'm moving here soon. My grandparents live nearby."

"You going to Carlisle?"

"Yeah. I think so."

"That's where most of us go."

We reached the other boys and Cory, apparently the organizer, got things under way.

"This is Foster," he said. "He's on our team. Blake, you take your guys to bat and we'll start off out here."

The taller, dark-haired kid named Blake headed toward home plate with his crew. Cory grabbed a glove off the ground and gave it to me. I slipped it on as he began sending people to their positions. Finally I was the only one left, and right field and pitcher were the last positions open. I assumed he was the pitcher.

He turned to me. "Can you pitch?" he asked.

I nodded.

He tossed me the ball and started for the outfield. I immediately regretted my decision. Suddenly I had a whole team of strangers watching me and counting on me. It had been a year since I'd pitched a baseball. I didn't think I'd ever do it again.

Blake was at bat. A right-hander. He looked like he knew what he was doing by the way he scraped the plate clean with his shoe and made a couple of test swings. Then he set up and locked eyes with me. I turned and assessed the field, noting everyone in position, getting a sense for distances.

"Put it in there," the center fielder said.

The catcher pounded his mitt.

Blake shifted his feet and set up again.

I took a deep breath and studied the catcher's mitt. I made my windup and let it go. Everything worked. It was fluid and easy and Blake's bat missed it by two inches. *Snap!* It was a strike.

"Dang!" Cory yelled.

The catcher threw it back to me and I caught it and couldn't help but smile.

27

When Mother found me we were four innings into the game, and I'd completely lost track of time. My pitching had us up 8–2 and my batting hadn't been bad either. The thing about it was I'd never been a standout pitcher before. I was good, but not this good. Either we had better baseball players in Baldwin County or I'd gotten better without practice. I didn't really care. Now they all knew my name.

"Foster!" she called from the fence.

I frowned and looked out at Cory. "I got to go," I called to him.

He started jogging my way and I waited until he reached me. "When you coming back?" he asked.

I took off the glove and put the ball in it and gave it to

him. "I don't know," I said. "Prob'ly some time later in the summer."

"Come find us again. We'll be out here."

"Okay," I said. "I'll see you around."

I could tell Mother was as surprised as me about the baseball game. "Looks like you made some friends already, Foster," she said.

I smiled and nodded, still high over it all.

"Well," she continued, "that's good. And baseball. Well, that's real good."

We visited Carlisle Middle School after eating lunch at my grandparents' house. A lady gave us a tour of the classrooms and the computer lab and library. It just seemed like another school to me, about the same size as the one I was leaving, just a different shape and different people. But it didn't hurt to imagine all the students like those I'd met at the park. And in my head I was already imagining myself as the star baseball player with all the friends.

"What did you think?" Mother asked me on the way home.

"Fine," I said.

"It looks like a good school."

I didn't know how you'd tell a good school from a bad one, but I knew enough to realize it wasn't really what she was asking me.

"I'm not worried about it," I said.

———

That evening Granddaddy sat in a chair next to the bed and read a story to me. He'd been doing it as long as I could remember. Even though I sometimes thought I was getting too old for it, I still enjoyed and looked forward to it. It was probably the one thing he did with me that stood out most.

Granddaddy's stories were ones I didn't hear in school—older tales from when he was young. Some of the first I remember are the *Just So Stories* by Rudyard Kipling, his favorite author. Then we'd gone on to Edgar Allan Poe and Daniel Defoe and Robert Louis Stevenson. That night we were on Kipling again. *The Strange Ride of Morrowbie Jukes*. It was long, but Granddaddy nearly had it memorized and skipped the slower parts so I could hear it all that night. When he was done, he set the book down and looked at me.

"That was the best story I ever heard," I said.

"Thought you'd be old enough for that one. I've got more."

I smiled and eased deeper under my covers.

"Heard you made some friends today," he said.

"Yes, sir."

"Must be that shiny bicycle."

I smiled again at his joke. He studied me for a moment without saying anything, like he was trying to read my thoughts. I turned away and stared at the ceiling.

"Foster," he finally said.

I looked at him again.

"You're going to be okay."

The way he said it reminded me that most days weren't and wouldn't be as good as today. It was almost a warning against becoming too complacent. I felt a knot rise in my throat and I swallowed against it.

"How do you know?" I asked.

"Because I've learned a lot of things in seventy-five years."

"Like what?"

"Life goes on. Wounds heal. Especially when you're young."

I took a deep breath and nodded. He got up and turned off the reading lamp and left the room. I faced the ceiling again and felt alone. The sounds of the baseball game were gone from my head and I didn't feel so good about anything anymore. Then my thoughts turned to Gary and I pictured him in the barn, leaning against the pack, reading his book with Kabo and Joe curled up not far away. What if we weren't supposed to leave the farm? Not after all those years—all that time Daddy spent building the place. How could we just leave it like it never meant anything? I didn't want to be in Montgomery. I wanted to go home.

28

When we pulled up to Fourmile I got out and ran around back. My anxiety eased when I saw Gary in the distance, standing in the truck bed and tossing hay over the back fence. Something caught my eye and I looked to the right to see Joe racing toward me from across the pasture. Kabo was on his heels and I knelt down to meet both of them. In a moment Joe was whining and rubbing against me and Kabo was beside him barking excitedly. I scratched both of them behind the ears and stood and the three of us set out toward Gary.

"Hey, stranger," he said.

"Hey, Gary. What are you doing?"

"Getting some of that old hay out of the barn."

I looked to the right and saw a long line of it scattered down the other side of the fence.

"It'll rot into the ground," he said.

"Mother wants you to come to supper."

He glanced at the house. "She does, does she?"

I nodded. "She wants me to bring the fish inside. You didn't eat it, did you?"

"No," he said, "I froze it, waiting on you."

"Good. She said it'll be about an hour."

He dropped the pitchfork into the truck bed and swung himself over the rail. He slapped the loose hay from his jeans, pulled off the bandanna, and wiped his face. "I better get cleaned up, then. Hop in and I'll give you a ride."

Gary parked the truck under the equipment shed and I followed him into the barn. I was surprised to see how neat the place was with most of the old hay gone. Now it smelled more of cedar and pine knot than moldy grass. It had a cool cavernous feel to it that was both refreshing and lonely at once.

"Looks different in here," I said.

"You think I swam in that creek all weekend?" he joked.

I smiled and shook my head.

Gary got the fish out of the freezer and gave it to me. "This should thaw out fast if we run some water over it," he said. He walked to his pack and pulled out a clean pair of jeans, boxer shorts, and a T-shirt. Then he grabbed his Dopp kit off the blanket and started toward the house.

"Where you going?" I asked.

"You don't mind if I use your shower, do you?" he said over his shoulder.

I didn't move. "My shower?"

"Yeah."

"No."

Gary was already knocking on the back door by the time I caught up to him. Mother opened it and I noticed she'd changed into fresh clothes.

"How was your trip?" he asked.

"It was nice, thank you. I think we made some progress."

"That's good," he said. "I hear I've got an invite to a fish dinner."

"We'd love to have you."

"I accept. Mind if I get cleaned up?"

"Not at all," she said, stepping aside. "You can use Foster's bathroom down the hall."

He went past her and I followed and pulled the kitchen door behind me. Mother went back to the counter where she was breaking snap beans. After a few seconds she looked at me.

"Well," she said. "Are you going to hand me the fish or just stand there?"

I sat down in front of the television, listening to my shower running down the hall, not watching whatever was on. It wasn't long before Gary returned, fresh-looking and re- laxed like he'd been that day at the creek. He walked into the living room and I saw Mother pass behind him and re- turn a moment later with his dirty clothes. He collapsed into the chair that Dax usually took, and put his hand through his hair that I suddenly realized was longer. I heard the washing machine start.

"You want to watch television?" I asked.

He glanced at the TV. "Go ahead," he said. "I'm going to nod off for a few minutes."

He tilted his head back and closed his eyes. I realized I'd never seen him shut his eyes. I turned off the television and watched him to see if he would wake, but he didn't.

She cooked the bass in the broiler and served it with buttered grits and the snap beans I'd seen her picking over at the counter. It was the best meal we'd had in a long time. She asked to say a blessing over the food, and I glanced at Gary to see if he was uncomfortable with it. He was already lowering his head like it was completely natural to him. I quickly did the same, but couldn't help glancing up at him before Mother was through. Then he started on his meal in an eager but polite way.

Mother told him about the houses she'd looked at and she asked me to tell him what I thought of the school I visited. I told him it was fine. I didn't want to talk about Montgomery. It had nothing to do with him.

"What are we going to work on tomorrow?" I asked.

"I figured we'd go into town and get the painting supplies. We'll spend a few days sanding and doing prep work."

Mother excused herself and got up to put Gary's clothes in the dryer.

"Did Joe do any tricks for you?"

"He almost ran an armadillo up my pants leg. If you call that a trick."

I sat up in my chair. "I told you he did that!"

"I put the stick on the fence post too."

"Did he get it?"

"I'm not sure he doesn't do a backflip on the way down."

I laughed. "He likes that one," I said. "You have to tell him to 'hold' or he'll get the stick before you can let go of it."

Mother returned and got her plate from the table. Gary looked at her and smiled. "I think we've got a fully recovered dog on our hands."

Mother glanced at me and looked at Gary. Her eyes were deep and wet in a way that I didn't understand. Much like the look I saw come over Granddaddy.

29

After supper I excused myself and left Gary and Mother at the table. I walked into my bathroom and looked about. I smelled it, searched for some trace of him. Other than a little condensation left on the shower door, it was as if he hadn't been there. I walked back into my room and stood in the middle of the floor listening.

"Did he come by?" I heard her ask.

"Yeah," he said.

"What'd he say?"

"I didn't talk to him. Joe started barking. By the time I walked around the house, he was driving off."

"I was afraid of that," she said.

"Phone's been ringing a lot too."

"I know," she said. "I had to unplug it a while ago . . . I'm sorry you had to get in the middle of things."

"It's no problem."

"Let me get your clothes for you," she said. "I think they're dry."

There was more silence. I heard a glass tap on the countertop in the kitchen. I moved closer to the wall, but stopped just short of it, feeling that somehow he knew I was listening.

"Here you go," I finally heard her say.

"I appreciate it. And thanks again for the meal."

"I meant what I said," she continued. "You're welcome to use the spare bedroom."

"I'm fine outside," he said. "I like it outside."

There was another moment of silence. Then Mother said something I couldn't hear.

"You just let me know," he said.

"I haven't seen him like this in a long time. He didn't used to do anything but lie in the barn with Joe."

I didn't hear Gary reply.

"Good night," she said.

"Good night, Linda."

She came into my room that night and sat beside me on the bed.

"I told him he could use your room before we left. I hope you don't mind."

"I don't mind," I said.

"I thought it was a good idea to have someone looking after the house."

"It's fine," I said.

She brushed my hair back with her fingers like she does when she has something to say but doesn't know how to say it.

"Let him stay," I said. "As long as he wants."

She sighed. "I like him too, Foster. But there's still a lot we don't know about Gary. There's a lot he doesn't want us to know. He's going to move on, and I can't tell you when that'll happen."

"But you don't have to be the one to make him."

"I think I've made it clear to him that he's welcome to stay for a while."

I nodded.

"Get some sleep," she said.

After she was gone I listened for the farm truck to crank, but the yard remained silent. Finally I knew he would have left if he was going. I closed my eyes and slept.

Gary and I started for town early the next morning. Mother was just getting into her car to head to work and we waved at her as we passed around the side of the house. The day was overcast and a line of squalls approached from the southwest.

"Where do you go at night?" I asked him.

"Sometimes I go into town."

"To get things?"

"Yeah. Sometimes I make phone calls."

"You could use the house phone."

"Sometimes it's pretty late."

"Mother's still up."

Gary looked at me and smiled. "Good thing we got that roof finished. Looks like the rain's on its way."

"You should move into the guest room," I said.

He looked at the road again. "Maybe I like it in the barn."

"It's hot out there."

"It's not closed up like a house," he said.

"And your dog couldn't stay with you."

He smiled again. "That's right. Joe and Kabo might get lonely."

"I wish I could sleep in the barn," I said.

"Ask your mother. I'm sure she wouldn't mind you camping out a few nights."

I looked out the window and smiled to myself.

We purchased sandpaper, brushes, paint, mineral spirits, and a drop cloth from the hardware store and headed back to Fourmile as the rain started coming down. We spent the day sanding the kitchen cabinets while thunder rumbled overhead. When Mother returned that afternoon we helped her carry groceries from the car and put them away. She invited Gary to supper again and he accepted.

Gary went out to the barn to get a change of clothes while I showered. When I was pulling on my shorts he knocked on my bedroom door and I told him to come in. He set a bundle of clothes on my bed and started undressing.

"Go help your mother," he said. "I'll be out in a few minutes."

30

We were halfway through dinner when I heard Joe barking and running around the house. I looked toward the front windows and saw headlights swinging across the yard. Gary was already scooting his chair back when I said, "Dax."

"*God!*" Mother said.

Gary walked down the hall to my bedroom and returned stuffing something into the back of his pants. He took a left and went into the living room and I saw the butt of the pistol visible just above his belt. He turned and sat on the sofa where he could see the front door. I started to get up and he gave me a look and shook his head.

Mother stood and went into the living room and stared out a front window.

"Just talk to him from the door," he said. "Don't go in the yard. I'll be right here."

Joe was barking in front of the house now. The headlights were stopped and shining onto the back wall.

"What about Joe?" I said.

"He'll be fine," Gary replied.

"Linda!" Dax yelled.

She opened the door and held her hands over her eyes. The headlights went out and the truck shut off. The only noise was Joe barking and leaping at Dax's window.

"Hey, baby," he said, like Joe wasn't even there. He'd been drinking again.

Mother lowered her hands. "Hi, Dax."

"Where you been?"

"Joe!" she snapped. "Stop that!"

Joe stopped barking, but he didn't move, and I heard rage vibrating in his throat.

"Visiting my parents," she said.

"That dog's gonna eat me yet," Dax said in a joking tone of voice.

"What do you want, Dax?"

"I just wanted to say I was sorry about everything. I got out of hand the other night. I was just worried about you."

Mother didn't say anything.

"How's Foster doin'? I thought I'd take him fishin' this weekend."

"I don't want to see you again, Dax," she said.

There was a period of silence.

"I don't want you to come over anymore," she continued. "And I don't want you calling me."

I heard his truck door creak and then Joe started barking.

"Damn," he said, shutting the door again. "Can't you at least get the dog out of my face?"

"Leave, Dax," she said.

"You're serious, aren't you?"

She didn't answer him.

"Who you got in there with you?"

"None of your business."

"He's in there, ain't he?"

She didn't answer him. I heard him spit.

"Fine," he said.

The truck cranked again. "That's fine, Linda," he continued. "Like I said, we ain't married. You go ahead and get him out of your system. You know where I live."

The headlights came on and moved across the wall then stopped. "And don't be surprised if I got company when you come over."

Once Dax was gone we returned to the table and tried to finish our meal. No one spoke. Gary was the only one eating while Mother and I picked at our food. Finally, Mother stood and excused herself. Gary nodded and watched her walk away. Then he turned to me. "Go ahead and finish," he said.

"You think that's it?"

"I hope so."

"She told him."

"I don't think he listens real good. It's late. Go ahead and eat and we'll walk out to the barn for a little bit."

31

I sat on a hay bale that he'd saved as a bench to set his things on. The dogs were sleeping at my feet and Gary was cleaning the pistol.

"Dax thinks you're Mother's boyfriend."

"Dax has got a drinking problem."

"Would you have shot him?"

"If what?"

"If he tried to hurt Mother."

"No."

"Why not?"

"It'd be enough just to show it to him."

"How come you have bullets in it?"

"I told you that already."

"Because you always have bullets in it?"

"That's right. And I'm not real comfortable with you being so curious over it."

"I won't touch it unless you tell me I can."

He glanced at me. "Good."

I wasn't sure how to take his tone of voice and I grew silent for a moment.

"Gary?" I said.

"Yeah."

"We've got a lot more to do, don't we?"

He kept wiping the pistol and didn't look up. "It'll take us a while to paint the cabinets and touch up some other places."

I took a deep breath. "What's after that?"

I noticed his hand stop for just a moment, then continue. "I don't know," he said. "I'll have to ask your mother."

"Why do you have to go to Texas?"

He smiled like the thought reminded him of something. Whether it had to do with my question or with that other thing he was always thinking of, I didn't know. He stopped wiping and wrapped the pistol in its cloth and set it into the pack. He dug around for a moment and pulled out a book and laid it before me. It was called *Coronado's Children* and I thought I recognized the general pattern of its cover as the one I'd seen him reading. I reached down and picked it up.

"My grandfather gave me this book when I was about your age," he said. "It's about lost treasure in the Southwest by a man named J. Frank Dobie. The way he tells the stories a person gets to thinking that maybe if they had enough time they could find the stuff. I've read everything he's written."

I looked up at him and his eyes were still on the book. His tone had softened and it immediately set me at ease.

"It's a foolish kind of thing to do," he said. "But I've got the time."

"Like gold?"

"Yeah," he said. "Spanish gold. Indian gold and silver."

"And you're going to go find it?"

He reached out and took the book from me. I was sorry I hadn't at least opened it to show I was interested. He dropped it back into the pack. "I figure I'm mostly going for a long walk into the desert," he said.

The way he said it—the distance it implied—the finality of it all filled me with a sudden rush of panic. "I don't want you to leave, Gary," I said.

He swallowed dry and looked away and didn't say anything.

"I want you to stay here," I said. "I want to stay here too. I didn't know before, now I do."

He stood and looked at the house and then down at Kabo. "I know, Foster . . . but it won't work."

Those words were everything I'd feared—everything I knew he'd say—the reason I never wanted to ask.

"She likes you," I blurted out. "I know she does!"

He looked at me and his lips were tight and for the first time he was completely removed from that other place in his head and entirely with me. "Foster," he said, "I know it seems to you like this thing has a simple answer, but it doesn't. I can't stay."

"Why!"

"I know it's not what you want to hear, but you won't appreciate it until you're older."

Suddenly I wished I'd never met him. Everything good he'd brought wasn't worth the hurt of what I was left with. "But you stayed this long," I said. "Why'd you do it? Why'd you come?"

He hesitated for a moment. "I didn't want this to happen," he said. "I should've left before now."

I jumped up and ran at him and hit him in the stomach as hard as I could. "Then why didn't you leave!" I yelled. I swung at him again and he stood there and took the blow, barely flinching. I was crying now and I felt sick. I swung at him again, weaker this time, and he grabbed my wrist lightly and held it there. I jerked it free and turned and ran out into the night. I kept on until I came to the pasture fence. I climbed over it and kept running for a few more yards until I stopped and collapsed and lay there sobbing with my cheek pressed to the wet grass and my eyes locked on the dark line of trees where my father was killed. Joe trotted up next to me and licked my face and I reached up and pulled him down and hugged him tight.

It seemed like I was lying there for a long time. A whip-poor-will called from the far tree line. As I listened for it, I thought I heard the lowing of a cow from some place far away. Suddenly his feet were before my face and it startled me enough to roll over. He sat beside me and put his hand on my shoulder.

"I don't want to talk about it anymore," I said.

He nodded. "You want to walk back to the house with me?"

I stood and wiped my face with the back of my hand. "I just want to walk back with Joe."

32

I woke the next morning and looked out my window. The farm truck was still there. Then I looked at the barn and caught a glimpse of him walking past the bay doors with Kabo following.

He didn't come for breakfast and I saw Mother occasionally glancing at the back door.

"Gary must not be hungry," she finally said.

She looked across the table at me when I didn't answer.

"Are you two painting today?"

I looked at my cereal. "I guess."

I could tell her eyes stayed on me. She knew something was wrong, but she didn't ask me about it. She took a deep breath and stood and grabbed her purse off the counter. "I've got to get to work," she said.

"Don't forget the dog food for Joe," I reminded her.

"Foster, just try the stuff I bought for him. The Champion Mix is really expensive."

"It's not good for him," I said flatly.

"Okay," she sighed. "I'll see if I can get some."

I waited until she was gone and got up with my cereal bowl and went to the sink. I dumped out what was left and couldn't help looking out the window. He was kneeling just outside the barn, stirring the paint.

"Good morning," he said.

"Morning."

"Could use some help today if you're up for it."

I looked at Joe. Back at Gary's hand stirring. I was ashamed he'd seen me crying. I was ashamed of everything. "Okay," I said.

Gary told me stories from the J. Frank Dobie book while we painted. Sometimes I asked him a question about something I didn't understand, but I mostly just listened, glad not to have to talk about what happened the night before. I knew everything was different now. And there was nothing either of us could say to change it.

He was ready to stop working earlier than usual that afternoon. Mother had not even returned from work by the time we took the brushes to the barn to clean them.

"I'm going to leave for a while tonight," he said.

"Why?"

"I have some things I need to do."

"But you'll come back?"

Gary smiled. "If I don't, they'll arrest me for stealing a truck."

I looked at the ground.

He put his hand on my shoulder. "Foster," he said.

I didn't answer him.

"I've been trying to think of a way to tell you some things."

I swallowed against the knot in my throat.

"I just need a little more time," he said.

"Okay," I said.

Gary drove off just after Mother returned from work. We ate alone that evening and then she went to her bedroom early. I walked out to the barn to check on Joe and saw that Gary had already fed him. I knelt and the two dogs came to me and I patted both of them while I studied the pack. After a few seconds I stood and walked over to it. I was scared to touch it. I knew he would know if I did. He knew exactly how he'd left it and how everything inside was arranged. Even though I'd heard him leave, just looking at it sent waves of fear up my back. Something told me he could be out there in the darkness watching me. Suddenly just appearing without a sound like he was able to do. I backed away from it and returned to the house.

I opened my eyes that night, not knowing what woke me. Then I heard Joe barking. I jumped out of bed and went to my window. The back of my neck tingled when I saw the farm truck missing. I ran to my bedroom door and found Mother in the hall.

"Stay in your room," she said, buttoning the top of her nightgown.

"He's not here," I said. "Gary's not here."

She swallowed and crossed her arms over her chest and started for the living room. Joe was still barking out front. I followed her to the end of the hall and stopped and watched her standing in the middle of the room. Headlights swiped across the wall and I heard the truck turn around in the yard and caught a glimpse of taillights headed out the driveway. Joe suddenly stopped barking.

"What's he doing?" I asked.

"I don't know," she said.

I went past her to the window and looked out. Dax's truck turned onto the highway and sped off. I saw Joe trotting away.

"Why'd he do that, Mother?"

She turned to me. "I don't know, Foster . . . But he's gone."

"I wish Gary was here."

She looked out the window again then back at me. Then she went over to the sideboard and opened the top drawer and pulled out Daddy's pistol, which I hadn't seen in a long time. She studied it.

"Do you know how to shoot it?" I asked.

She turned and looked at me like she'd forgotten I was standing there. Then she put the pistol back into the drawer and shut it. "I told you to stay in your room," she said.

"What are you going to do?"

"I'm going to stay up until Gary gets back. Now go. I don't want to tell you again."

I lay awake until I heard the farm truck pull around the house. I jumped out of bed and ran to the window as Gary parked under the equipment shed. Kabo was already out of the barn and racing around the truck. I heard the back door shut and saw Mother walking across the yard, dangling the pistol in her hand.

Gary knelt behind the truck and petted Kabo, then stood and waited for her. Then I saw them talking and he took the pistol from her and looked at it and gave it back. They talked some more until Mother finally turned and headed for the house.

Gary watched after her until I heard the door shut. Then he started for the barn with Kabo beside him. I left the window and went to my bedroom door and opened it just as Mother was passing. She no longer had the pistol in her hand and she seemed more relaxed.

"What's he going to do?" I asked.

"He's going to talk to him if he comes by again."

"What if he's not here like tonight?"

"Then I'll call the police. Everything's going to be fine. Go on to bed."

"I want to go see him."

"It's two o'clock in the morning. No."

I frowned and went back to my room. I got my knife and lay in bed, staring at the ceiling fan, squeezing the hilt in my palm, imagining the terror of Dax's goat face pressed against my window. I heard Mother's bedroom door close and I squeezed the knife and it didn't comfort me like I wanted it to. I got out of bed and walked quietly into the living room and opened the top drawer of the sideboard. The pistol was there looking heavy and deadly. I lifted it out and closed the drawer.

33

I woke to the sound of Mother talking in the kitchen. I slowly pulled myself from a groggy sleep and realized that the sunlight was strong through the window. I'd slept later than usual.

I sat up and rubbed my eyes and listened. I heard Gary's voice.

"Go on to work," he said. "I'll handle it."

"Oh God, Gary. I can't leave."

"You're late already. There's nothing you can do."

"Can't we take him somewhere?"

"No. I've seen it before. You'll spend a lot of money with the same result."

"It's going to crush him, Gary."

He didn't answer. I still didn't know what they were talking about.

"Go on, Linda," he said.

"Oh God," she said again. "Okay. Oh God."

I got out of bed and walked to the center of the floor. I heard the front door shut and I wanted to go out and see Gary, but not so fast that they might know I was listening. I heard him get a glass from the kitchen cabinet and then the sink came on. I walked slowly into the hall and down it until I could see into the kitchen. The glass of water was beside him and he was leaning over with his elbows on the counter and his forehead in his hands.

"Hey, Gary," I said.

He straightened and faced me. His eyes were red like he hadn't been sleeping. "Hey, Foster."

"What are you doing?"

He swallowed against something he didn't want to say. "I need your help in the barn this morning," he said. "Joe's sick."

Everything I'd heard came suddenly rushing over me and all the pieces fell into place. Buzzing rose in my ears and my breathing went shallow.

"He ate something bad last night."

There was only one question that sat in my head. "Is he going to die?"

Gary studied me for what seemed like forever. "Yes," he said. "I think so."

I started for the back door and felt the tears coming. I wiped my face and kept on across the yard toward the barn door, a big, dark, open mouth before me. I couldn't hear anything, taste anything, smell anything. My senses were numb to the world.

I found Joe lying on Gary's blanket, his tongue protruding and clamped between his teeth, bared ugly and mean like it wasn't him inside at all. His stomach rose and fell in quick bursts. Yellow bile was puddled around his face and the blanket was stained with a dark, bloody substance behind his legs. I sat beside him and put my hand on his head. The one eye facing up stared at some place in the beams overhead.

"Joe?" I said.

I leaned over to get into his line of sight and thought I saw the pupil twitch the slightest bit. I fell across him and sobbed into his neck fur. "No," I cried. "Don't die, Joe. Please don't die."

I felt Gary's hand on my back.

I squeezed Joe tighter and felt the small convulsions passing through him like electricity. "We have to help him!" I said. "We have to do something!"

"He's poisoned, Foster. His liver's shut down."

I sat up, pried his teeth open, and tried to get his tongue back in. It was cold and thick and limp. It kept falling out until I held it against the base of his mouth and let the jaws snap shut.

"We need to take him to the vet, Gary!"

"He's going to die, Foster. Probably before we can get there."

Joe spasmed and gagged and the tongue flopped out

again. I started trying to stuff it back into his mouth, but Joe kept gagging and it kept falling out. Gary grabbed my arm. "Stop, Foster."

"Make his tongue stop doing that, Gary!"

"You're not helping him!"

I fought against him. "You're not either!" I yelled.

"If we could make it to a vet, he'd die alone in a back room. I think you'd regret not being with him."

I stopped struggling and relaxed. Gary let go of my arm and put his hand on my shoulder. I lay across my dog again and squeezed him and cried.

I stayed with him until my cheek no longer felt the twitching in his stomach. Only an hour had passed, but it felt like longer. Gary was still sitting quietly behind me with Kabo. I sat up and my face felt dry and tight. I looked at Joe's face and the sight of the tongue made me sick and I crawled away and puked onto the ground. Then I lay on my side, facing the house. "He was fine last night," I mumbled.

"I found him at the back door this morning," Gary said.

"He was fine last night," I said again.

"When did you last see him?"

"He barked at Dax. I saw him run around the house after Dax left."

Gary's feet passed my face. "I'll be back in a minute," he said.

I watched him cross the yard and angle out of sight

around the house. I lay there, breathing, not ever wanting to move again. After a few minutes Gary returned. I saw him holding his knife at his side with something stabbed onto the end of it. He passed me and then I heard him getting something from the toolroom. After a few seconds he was standing over me. "Come on," he said. "Take this and I'll carry Joe."

I sat up and took the shovel from him. I turned and watched as he wrapped Joe in the blanket and stood with him cradled in his arms. "Where do you think he'd like to be?" he asked me.

I knew where Joe wanted to be. The place where he found me. The place where we built tree forts and paths through the woods. Where we swam in the creek. Where my father was killed. And now, in a numb way, I was no longer scared.

I stood. "In the woods at the back of the pasture," I said.

"Okay," Gary said. "We'll take the truck."

We drove through the back gate with Joe in the truck bed. We bumped across the pasture and my head swayed and my eyes stayed focused on the tall canopy of trees that held the back sixty acres of creek bottom.

"I want to tell you what happened," I said.

I saw Gary look over at me.

"About Daddy," I said.

34

I let the memories come flooding over me, filling my head like a liquid nightmare. Black fluid poison. Flashes, dappled sunlight, barking, running, yelling. Everything that had been pooled inside me for a year.

"There's a creek back there," I said. "It's in a gully. Daddy helped me build a tree fort a long time ago. Last year we were gonna build a bridge over the creek so we could hunt Mr. Hixon's woods. He has woods that go for almost a mile. And he's got a pasture with cows and mules. Now our cows are there too. Daddy tried to cut down a tree so that it would fall over and we could walk across it. He cut it with his chain saw and it got stuck in another tree. He told me to stay back, so I was in the fort with Joe because he could climb ladders. Daddy was pushing on the tree, trying to get it loose. I heard something snap and then all these branches and leaves were coming down. When everything stopped I couldn't see him. I came down and he was under the tree. It fell on him."

"Jesus," Gary mumbled.

"He tried to tell me what to do, but I couldn't understand him. The tree covered him up so all I could see was the side of his head in the leaves. There was blood around his head. I couldn't move the tree. I couldn't understand him."

The forest in front of us was growing closer and taller. "There was nothing you could have done, Foster."

"I couldn't understand what he was saying."

"It was too big."

Suddenly I knew Gary didn't know any more than the rest of them. No more than Mother. No more than Granddaddy. None of them knew the answers to anything. I was alone with it all and there was no sense in holding any of it back until the right person came along to take it away. It was just this and it would always be this and it would sit in me and rot my guts.

"There's an opening in the trees up there," I said. "You can drive into it a little ways."

He kept on to the tree line and found the opening and we plunged into the dark shade of the creek bottom. We drove until we came to the end of where Daddy had Bush Hogged the year before.

Gary shut off the truck and we got out and I grabbed the

shovel while he lifted the blanket with Joe in it. He looked at me and motioned with his chin for me to lead. I started past him.

"You okay?" he asked.

"I think Joe lived in the woods before he found me," I said.

The gum trees and water oaks towered overhead and the leafy damp of the forest floor was like a smell from another time long ago, instantly familiar but something I'd given up and had no place for. Birds flitted through the forest canopy and a cardinal made its shrill whistle that brought to mind the smell of sawdust and chalky nails and sawn cypress and anticipation.

The pieces of the giant gum tree came into view. It had been cut into several sections by the firemen and pulled about. Part of it had rolled into the gully and the top half stuck up on the opposite slope, brittle and dead. To my left was the tree fort. I stopped and faced it. The roof was littered with Spanish moss and tree limbs. The boards were green with algae. But it was there, hanging in the trees like dried bones. I knew that if I climbed up to it I would know the feel of every board under my palms and my ankles would adjust to every tilt and slant and I would move up the ladder on muscle memory alone and swing into the fort and lie on my back and know every knothole and grain pattern of every board on the under-side of the ceiling. But I had no desire to climb the dead thing. I looked at the gully again.

"Right here," I said.

We buried Joe and left him there. We drove back across the pasture and to the house without speaking. It wasn't until we were stopped beside the barn that I looked at Gary and realized he was lost in his own thoughts.

"Stay here," he said.

He got out and took the shovel from the truck bed. He disappeared into the barn and came back and got into the truck with the knife and what I now recognized as a small piece of meat stabbed on the end of it.

"You eat steak last night?" he asked me.

"No."

He cranked the truck and started around the side of the house.

"You know where he lives?"

"Who?"

"Dax."

"I've been there once."

His jaw tightened as he shifted into second gear. "Show me the way."

35

I told Gary to turn left out of the driveway. He swung onto the blacktop and shifted into third gear, staring straight ahead. I looked at the piece of meat lying skewered on the dashboard. It was the size of a card deck and covered with dirt and grass. I saw where half of it had been torn away. It looked harmless.

"You think that was it?" I asked.

"Yeah," he said.

"You think Dax did it?"

"Yeah."

"What are you going to do to him?"

He didn't answer me.

"Did you bring your pistol?"

"No."

"Why not?"

He turned to me. "When we get there I want you to stay in the truck."

I nodded and he looked at the road again. We didn't talk until he came to the fourway. "Left," I said.

We kept on through the farmland and into Robertsdale. We slowed at the one caution light, passed under, and continued a few more miles outside of town. Finally we passed the metal fabrication shop that I remembered as a landmark. I pointed to the red clay road on the right. Gary downshifted and made the turn and we were suddenly walled in by the pine plantation.

"It's not far now," I said.

We went around the first bend and I pointed to Dax's house on the left. Gary came to a stop in the road and studied it.

"Truck's gone," he said.

"He's got a shop in the back where he mounts deer heads and stuff. It might be back there."

Gary glanced in the rearview mirror then looked at me. "Remember what I told you?"

I nodded.

He put the truck in gear and eased forward. "Good," he said.

Gary swung around in the front yard and parked with the truck pointed out the driveway. He shut it off, grabbed the piece of poisoned meat, and got out. He stood studying the house. I heard crows calling in the distance and the shadow of a buzzard swiped across the hood. The engine hissed and ticked in the silence.

"I'm going to walk around back," he finally said. "Stay put."

I turned sideways in my seat and watched him through the rear glass. He angled across the yard, keeping his eyes on the dark windows of the house. Once he rounded the corner, he straightened his posture and picked up his pace like he'd seen something that put him in a hurry. I slid over to the driver's side and craned my head out the window, but I lost sight of him.

Minutes passed as the crow calls moved into the distance and the engine cooled and ticked out. I strained my ears, but there was nothing else. Not a dog barking, not a car on the empty road, nothing. Then suddenly I heard what sounded like a hammer hitting a piece of sheet tin. It was quickly followed by the sound of lumber snapping. All of it coming from behind the house. I felt a surge of panic bolt through me and I looked out at the empty road and back again. I started to grab the door handle, then remembered what Gary told me and drew my hand back.

I waited, watching the side of the yard where I'd last seen him. After a few minutes I thought I saw something flash across the house window and my eyes darted to the place and stayed there. I felt my heart beating through my temples.

"Gary," I whispered.

The front door cracked slightly and hung there. Then it swung all the way open and Gary stepped onto the porch and looked at me. I let out a deep breath and eased lower in my seat. He left the door open and took a few steps into the yard before turning and looking back. I saw that his shirt was torn and noticed that his bandanna was gone. He started my way again, moving quickly, staring at the ground. When he slid onto the driver's seat I saw his entire right arm was covered in blood.

"Gary!"

He leaned forward and used his left hand to pull his shirt over his head. Then he draped it over the bloody arm.

"Tie the sleeves tight just above my elbow," he said.

I scooted over and took the two sleeves and began to fumble with them.

"Come on," he said. "Hurry up."

I focused and pulled a half hitch snug just below his biceps. He glanced at it.

"Tighter," he said.

I grabbed the sleeves again and pulled them harder. He moved the arm away and turned the ignition and blood fell onto his knee and shoes. I looked at him and his face was tight and strained.

"What happened?"

He dropped his arm to his side and popped the clutch, the truck leaping forward. He had the truck redlined in first gear until we'd made the turn onto the dirt road. Then I heard the creak of the clutch spring again.

"Push the column shifter up for me," he said.

I leaned over and shoved the shifter up. He let out the clutch pedal and we lurched ahead in second gear.

He shoved the clutch in again. "Third," he said.

I pulled it down into third gear. The pine trees flashed by outside my window and red dust rose in a cloud behind us.

"What happened, Gary?"

"He cut me with an arrow. I'll be okay."

"He shot you with it?"

"No, he just cut me with it."

"What'd you go in his house for?"

He didn't answer me. We barely slowed at the blacktop before leaning into a hard turn. Gary straightened the truck and gunned it.

"Gary?"

"I shouldn't have brought you," he said. "It was stupid of me."

"What'd you do to him?"

He kept his eyes on the road. "That's enough questions, Foster. I've got to concentrate and I need you to stay ready on the gearshift."

36

He stood at the kitchen sink, letting the tap run hot over his arm and fill the basin with water that looked like cherry Kool-Aid. I got some paper towels for him and brought them over. I saw the cut, a deep slice on the underside of his arm from wrist to elbow. The sight of it made me queasy and I turned away and stared at the floor.

"Call your mother," he said. "Tell her to come home."

I went to the phone and picked it up and there was no dial tone.

"Plug it in," he said.

I connected it to the wall and dialed Mother at the post office.

"Mother," I said.

"I'm so sorry about Joe, Foster. I'm—"

"Gary's hurt," I said. "We need you to come home."

"I need you to find some things for me while we wait on her," he said. "You need to hurry because I'm not going to be able to stand up much longer."

"Okay," I said.

"First, I want you to find some rubbing alcohol. Open it on the way back."

I went into Mother's bathroom and got the alcohol and brought it back to him open. He took it and held his arm over the sink and poured the entire bottle over it. Then he dropped the bottle and looked away and lowered his head and I saw his neck muscles rise. He made a sound from somewhere deep in his throat and leaned on his left elbow. There was blood everywhere now. The counter, the sink, his pants, the floor.

"Go get a towel and some tape," he stammered.

"What—"

"Any kind. Start it for me."

I ran and got a towel out of the bathroom and some duct tape out of the kitchen drawer. I lifted a corner of it and walked up behind him. He straightened and held his hand back to me and I put the tape in it.

"Wrap the towel tight around my arm."

I did what he said and held it. Blood was already wicking through the white cloth. He bit the tape end and pulled out a length. He dragged it over the towel and dropped the spool. Then he reached under and grabbed it where it swung and threw it over again. He did this several times until the towel was secured.

"Tear it," he said.

I leaned over and bit it and tore the spool free. He lowered himself to the floor and sat there with his eyes closed, breathing deep, the arm limp in his lap.

"Gary?" I said.

He didn't answer me.

"Gary!"

He opened his eyes and cocked them up at me.

"You're not going to die, are you?"

He cracked a smile and shook his head. I didn't believe him.

"Don't close your eyes," I said.

"I told you I'd be okay," he replied. "I've lost a lot of blood. I'm just a little weak."

"Why don't we call an ambulance?"

He shook his head. "I'm okay. I just need to sit here. Just stop talking to me for a while."

I heard Mother's car drive up and I was halfway to the front door by the time she came bursting in.

"What happened!" she said.

"Dax cut Gary's arm. He's on the kitchen floor."

She brushed past me and I chased after her into the kitchen. I saw her look horrified at his arm.

"Gary!"

He looked up at her. "I'm okay," he said. "Call the police and file a report."

She knelt beside him and started to lift on his good arm. "We need to get you to a doctor."

He pulled the arm down. "Don't call the doctor, Linda. Don't argue with me about that. Call the police and file a report. Tell them what Dax did to Joe last night. Tell them you're scared."

"What if they want to come here?"

"They probably will. Don't mention me."

"What happened, Gary?"

"Just do it, Linda. Then we'll talk about the rest. No doctors."

She started to say something but didn't. Finally she nodded and stood and hurried to her bedroom. I stayed with Gary while she made the phone call. She came back and stood over him.

"They're coming over," she said. "They need to make a report."

He nodded slowly. "Take me to Foster's room so I can lie down."

"Is he going to be okay, Mother?"

"Quiet, Foster," she said. "I want you to start cleaning up this kitchen. I want it done fast. All the blood on the floor. Anywhere there's blood."

"You don't have to invite them inside, Linda."

"It makes me too nervous," she said.

He nodded. "You're right," he mumbled. "Foster, drive the truck under the equipment shed after you're finished."

I started for the paper towels.

Mother took Gary down the hall and returned a few minutes later. She helped me clean the blood from the sink and the counter and the floor and the walls. Then she sent me outside to move the truck and spray off the back stoop with the hose.

When I was finished out back I went to my room and changed out of my bloody clothes. Then I walked into the kitchen just as the police began knocking on the door.

"Go back to your room and wait for me," she said.

I walked into my room and saw that Gary wasn't there. I heard Mother opening the front door and the voices of men. I backed out and went into Mother's room and saw him in her bed lying on his back with his eyes closed. I pulled the door behind me and approached him. He opened his eyes and smiled at me. Then he put a finger to his lips. "I'm all right," he said softly.

I felt myself starting to cry again all of a sudden. It was like something shaken up from inside me. I tried to swallow it away, but I was choking against it.

"Shhh," he said.

I put my hand over my mouth and coughed and nodded, but I couldn't stop the tears.

"Come here," he said.

I felt like my legs were about to give out and I felt light-headed.

"Foster," he said. "Come lie down."

I crawled onto the bed and lay on my side facing him, coughing against my palm and trembling. He took his good hand and reached across himself and stroked my hair. "You did good," he said.

I hugged him and cried into his shirt.

37

It wasn't until Mother stood over us that I realized the sound of the men talking had stopped. She touched my shoulder, but I didn't move. Finally she nudged me and I rolled over and looked at her. She was holding a box of dental floss and a sewing needle.

"I need to see his arm, Foster."

I scooted to the end of the bed. I thought she would tell me to leave, but she didn't. She sat down beside him and crossed her legs and started to gently peel off the duct tape. He stared at the ceiling fan.

"I don't know anything about this," she said.

"There's not much to it," he replied. "I've already cleaned it."

"Tell me if I hurt you."

He glanced at the arm, then looked at me, then looked at the ceiling fan again. "Dax poisoned the dog," he said. "I went to talk to him about it. Things got out of hand."

She got the tape off and unfolded the towel. I saw her face go ashen. She swallowed and looked away and fumbled with the dental floss.

"You can't worry about hurting me," he said. "You've just got to sew it up before I lose any more blood."

"Go get another towel, Foster," she said.

I got up and went into her bathroom to get a towel.

"You shouldn't have taken him," I heard her say.

"I know. I shouldn't have . . . I didn't expect it to go like it did."

"Should I be scared?"

"Of Dax?"

I didn't hear her reply.

"We don't need to worry about him for a while," he said. "He's in pretty bad shape."

I came back with the towel and gave it to her. The cut was separating and blood rose into the valley of the cut like a spring boil. She put the towel under it and began threading the needle.

"I'm going to see it through," he said. "It'll be all right."

She held the needle and thread over his arm and studied the wound. She took a deep breath.

"Start near my wrist," he said. "I think it's deepest there."

"What if it cut something important?" she said. "What if there's something in there that needs to be fixed?"

"I can make a fist. I think everything works."

"Okay," she said. "Here I go."

She leaned over and closed the lip of the wound with her fingers. Blood ran over the sides of his arm. She glanced at him, but his face held no expression. She ran the needle through and pulled the floss to the knot at the end. He didn't flinch.

"All right?" she asked.

"Keep going."

She ran the needle through again and pulled the first suture snug. Then she had more confidence and made steady progress up the arm.

"How did it happen?" she asked.

"He stabbed at me with a hunting arrow. I tried to grab it and it slid through my hands."

She winced and kept working. Eventually there was what looked like a tiny, waxy white railroad track in a mess of blood. Then she took the edge of the towel and blotted most of it clean.

"Go get some alcohol, Foster," she said.

"I think we used it all."

"I've got a brown bottle of hydrogen peroxide in my bathroom drawer. Go get that."

I left again.

"What makes you so sure he won't come tonight, Gary?" I heard her ask.

"I ripped some wires out of his truck and cut his phone line. It's going to take him a while to crawl up that dirt road and get some help."

"Crawl?"

"I beat him senseless," he said with no remorse. "I had to stop myself. I wanted to kill him."

Silence.

"He's got friends," she said.

"I've seen them."

I returned with the bottle. She poured a thin line down the track of sutures and it rose and bubbled white. After a few seconds she dabbed it dry and got up and went into the bathroom. I heard the sink come on and in a minute she came back wiping her hands on a washcloth.

"Okay." She sighed. "What next?"

"Go get my pistol, Foster."

I looked at Mother and she moved her chin for me to go on. I left the room and went outside into a twilight that was quieter than any I remembered. Kabo rose from the back stoop and looked at me with a question. I reached down and scratched him behind the ears. "He's all right, boy," I said. Then it hit me that Joe was gone. And it seemed like something that had happened a long time ago—something that wasn't even real. But the pain of it was so mixed in with everything else that it fell flat and was impossible to dwell on.

I got the pistol out of his pack and brought it back to

him. Mother was still standing where I'd left her and I could tell they'd been talking about something. I put the pistol on the bed and he reached across his stomach and took it.

"Let's go, Foster," Mother said. "Gary needs to rest."

38

I followed her into the kitchen. She opened the refrigerator and started pulling out leftovers. "Go into your room and pack some clothes," she said. "We're going to Granddaddy's tonight."

"What?"

She straightened and looked at me. "You heard what I said, Foster. Please just do what I say. I'm really tired."

I slowly shook my head.

"Foster," she warned, "now's not the time for this."

"We're not leaving him here like that."

"Go pack your clothes," she said again.

"He won't be here when we get back."

"Yes he will."

"No he won't! And you know it!"

She took a step toward me. I turned and bolted out the back door.

"Foster!" she yelled.

I kept running until I was in front of the barn and turned and walked backward, facing the house. She stood in the doorway watching me. She rubbed her hand over her face with frustration. I turned and went through the bay doors and lay down in the dirt next to his pack. Kabo trotted up and settled next to me and whined from deep in his throat. The refrigerator clacked and hummed from the far corner and the moths darted about the overhead bulb. It was so empty.

"Daddy," I said. "I don't know what to do. I don't wanna leave you. I don't know if you're still here."

But there was nothing except the whisper of a light breeze in the pecan orchard and the grit against my face.

"I just want you to come back," I said. "That's all I want."

It rained that night and a breeze swept cool mist through the bay doors. I was so wound up that I couldn't sleep. I kept opening my eyes and watching the house, Kabo breathing heavily beside me. The lights in the kitchen were still on, but I hadn't seen her pass the window.

Finally, I must have slept. I woke later that night to Kabo whining and standing up. Mother was hurrying across the yard with a rain jacket over her head. I'd thought she wouldn't come after me. She hadn't been in the barn in a year.

I sat up and crossed my legs and waited for her. She stepped inside and lowered the rain jacket and studied me. I didn't say anything.

She looked around and saw a nail on the wall and went and hung the jacket on it. Then she turned and looked around again.

"It's been a long time since I've been in here," she said.

"I know."

She walked over and sat down beside me. Kabo resettled in his spot and she petted him with her other hand.

"It smells like his clothes in here," she said.

"I know."

"Gary said you took him to the ravine today."

I nodded. "We buried Joe back there."

She didn't say anything for a moment. "I miss him too, Foster," she said. "I don't know when it stops."

"I don't think it does," I said.

"I just wish I had the answer to a lot of things."

"Nobody has the answers," I said.

"You can't want to stay here," she said. "He's just not here now."

"But Gary is."

She looked at me and sighed. "I told you not to get attached to him. I told you he was leaving."

"You got attached to him."

She looked away.

"You know he's in trouble," I said. "And you let him stay."

"I don't know any more about him than you, Foster."

"Why won't he see doctors? Why is he scared of the police? He looks around all the time like people are after him."

She looked at Kabo and didn't answer me.

"Why?" I asked again.

"I don't know," she finally said. "I keep thinking tomorrow's the day he'll be gone. And I can stop thinking about him. I don't trust my decisions these days, Foster."

"I don't want to go to Montgomery," I said. "I won't. Not yet."

"Well, it's too late to leave now. But Gary says you can't stay out here tonight."

"He's awake?"

"He was. But he's probably asleep again and you're not going to bother him."

"Does he think Dax'll come tonight?"

She shook her head. "He doesn't think so. But the barn's no place to be if he does."

"Mother?"

"Yes."

"Why can't we just fix it all?"

She pulled me close and rocked against me. "I'm trying, Foster. I'm trying."

39

I woke in my bed the next morning to the smell of bacon cooking. The storm had moved on and sunlight came softly through the curtains and fell over my face. I heard Mother on the phone, telling the post office that she wasn't going to come in that day. I got out of bed, walked down the hall, and peered into her room. Gary cocked his eyes at me and smiled his crooked smile.

"Morning," he said.

I opened the door and walked to the bed and sat on it. His arm was wrapped in gauze strips and a line of blood showed through. "Does it still hurt?" I asked him.

"Yeah," he said.

"How long are you going to have to lie here?"

"You ready to get back to work?" he joked.

I smiled weakly. "No. I just wondered."

"What'd I tell you about doing what your mother says?"

I looked at my hands and didn't answer him.

"Hey," he said.

I looked at him.

"I told her you needed to get out of town last night."

"I'm not going," I said.

He studied me for moment. Then, for the first time, it was him that turned away. He looked at the ceiling. "Thanks for showing me your tree fort yesterday, Foster."

"I was fine because you were with me."

He looked at me again. "You were fine because there's nothing to be scared of. You get scared of life and it's got you beat."

"Sometimes I wonder if our cows know how close they are to where they used to live."

He watched me.

"They probably like having the mules," I said. "We never had mules."

He listened patiently.

"Mules chase coyotes away from the calves."

"I didn't know that."

I nodded. "They hate coyotes. That's why farmers have them."

"Sounds like a good place to be for a cow."

"Yeah," I said.

"I smell bacon," he said. "Been a while since I've had breakfast in bed."

"When does your blood grow back?"

"Couple of weeks. Maybe a month."

My eyes widened.

He smiled. "I won't be in bed that long," he said. "I'm going to get up and walk around some today. Just might be a little dizzy for a while."

"I can paint until you're better."

"It'll wait," he said. "Why don't you go out to the barn and get the rest of my things and bring them inside. Put them in your room."

"Okay," I said.

"That pack's pretty heavy."

I got up to leave. "I can get it," I said.

I walked into the barn and saw Kabo lying next to Gary's pack. I got some of Joe's dog food and poured it into his bowl and made the clicking sound. I could tell he'd lost some of his spirit too. He got up and slunk to the bowl with his head down. He looked at it then looked up at me again.

"I know, boy," I said. "Me too."

I gathered Gary's things and put them into the pack. I hefted it onto my shoulder and staggered toward the house with it. After I got it to my room, I went back to the kitchen, where Mother had bacon and eggs and biscuits ready. She fixed a plate for me and a TV tray for Gary. She knew what I was thinking.

"Let him eat in peace, Foster," she said.

I took my plate to the dining room table and watched her disappear with Gary's tray. In a few minutes she came back to the kitchen and started cleaning up. I finished eating and took my plate and eased it around her into the sink.

"I took off work," she said. "I can't leave you here with him like that."

"Dax'll try to kill him."

She turned to me. "If Dax tries to come over, then I can call the police and have him arrested."

"Then we can't leave. We have to watch for him."

She studied me for a moment then turned back to the sink.

"No reason we need to stay cooped up in this house all day," I heard Gary say.

We both turned and saw him leaning against the wall. His face was pale and his bandaged arm hung limp and swollen at his side.

"Are you okay?" she asked.

"Little light-headed. Like I've got a blowtorch on my arm."

"Maybe you should rest some more," she said.

"If you can wrap it in a plastic bag for me I think a soak in the creek might get my fever down."

"I can fix a bath for you."

"A little sunshine and fresh air wouldn't hurt either."

"You don't think we should be here?"

He hesitated and gave her a long look. "I think it'd do us all some good to get away for the day."

40

I loaded Kabo in the truck, feeling the stab of Joe's memory once again. But it was like a loss that was partly on hold while something bigger hung over me. I slammed the tailgate and blocked it away.

I drove around to the front of the house and saw Mother coming out, holding Gary by his good arm. He didn't seem to need the help, but took it anyway. I scooted over and opened the door for him, and Mother waited until he'd eased himself onto the seat. Once he was settled she shut the door and went back inside. She came back a moment later with an ice cooler and a cloth bag and put them in back with Kabo. Then she got behind the wheel and studied the column shifter and smiled like there was something she'd been holding back. "Been a while since I've driven one of these," she said.

"Want to help her out, Foster?"

I leaned over and started to grab the gear lever.

"Now, hold on," she said. "I was driving these things ten years before you were born."

"I've never seen you," I said.

"Well, sit back in your seat. I used to do more than wash dishes and sort mail."

I looked at Gary and he stared ahead and smiled.

She could drive it. We sputtered and jerked in the driveway, but once she got on the blacktop, she was working through the gears as good as anybody I'd seen. It was just cloudy enough so that large shadows eased across the pastureland and the morning alternated between sunlight and shadow. It felt good to leave Fourmile. It felt good to let go of it all and put it down for just a little while. I was getting tired now. Tired of thinking about everything. Tired of clinging to everything.

She spread a blanket on the creek bank and Gary eased himself onto it. She sat next to him and got a garbage bag and taped it over his arm. I sucked in my stomach and crossed my arms and waded into the creek. When I turned, Gary was sliding on his rear into the shallows. He came to rest with his good elbow propped on tree roots and the water swirling around his torso.

"Far as I go today," he said.

"Feels good," I lied.

He laid his head back and looked into the cool canopy of the evergreens. Kabo walked up behind him and settled down just above his head.

"I'm going to catch a fish," I said.

"Get dinner for us," he replied.

I lowered my arms and started wading downstream. I hadn't gone far when I felt loneliness creeping over me. I slowed and studied the shaded tunnel of juniper and cypress curving out of sight. Suddenly I didn't want to go and I stopped and looked back. I couldn't see them behind the trees. I was ashamed. I stepped over to the edge of the creek bank and sat down in the shallows and wedged myself between two cypress trees. A breeze rustled overhead and their voices came clear over the gurgling water.

"Would you tell me if I asked?" she said.

He didn't reply right away. Then I heard him say, "No."

"Do I want to know?"

"You don't need to be scared of me," he said. "It's nothing for you to be scared of."

"I'm not scared of you. Not in that way."

He didn't answer.

"What do you think will happen to you?" she finally said.

"I don't know."

"Was it just a mistake?"

"No, it wasn't a mistake. I knew what I was doing."

"But you're a good person."

"Am I? Why did I stay? If I was such a good person, I would have left."

"You know why," she said.

"You could go to prison, Linda."

No one spoke for a moment. For the first time I wondered where Mother had slept the night before.

"I just needed somebody," she said. "I didn't know he was like that."

"You've got some bad luck when it comes to men."

"Foster's dad was as good as they come. He always did the right thing. I don't consider any part of him bad luck."

"I didn't mean it like that."

"I know," she said. "You remind me of him."

"But I don't always do the right thing."

"You can have the truck," she said.

"I can't drive with this arm."

"Maybe a lawyer can help?"

"Even if I had the money, no lawyer can help. There's no defense against what I did."

She sounded desperate. "I can drive you somewhere. Get you a hotel room for a while. I can pay for that."

"Forget it, Linda. Unless you get everything in that house packed today, I'm not going anywhere. I'm telling you, Dax is no joke. And I can assure you he's into more than power lines and cutting up dead animals."

"But he works for the power company. He can't have a criminal record."

"He doesn't work for the power company, Linda."

"But—"

"He does contract work for his buddy's trenching service. They do some jobs for the power company."

She didn't say anything.

"And you don't dig trenches at night," he said.

"How do you—"

"I called the power company and asked about him," he said.

She didn't reply.

"You were vulnerable," he said.

"It's no excuse."

"Yes it is. But I'm going to see this through for you."

"What can you do with your arm like that?"

"Enough. I'm better already."

"Maybe he'll leave us alone." She sighed.

"I don't think so."

I sat there frozen, too scared to move. Scared they'd see in my face that I'd been listening. I realized I was shivering and it seemed like maybe I'd been shivering for a while. They had stopped talking. I stood and waded quietly downstream and stopped and waited a few minutes more. Then I grabbed a stick and hit it against a tree and started back toward them, being as loud as I could. When they came into sight Gary was lying on his back on the blanket and Mother was sitting up watching for me. Her eyes were red and her mouth was drawn tight.

"Did you get anything?" she asked me.

I shook my head.

"I told you it takes practice," Gary said to the sky.

"Come on up, Foster," she said. "You look like you're freezing."

After lunch we went riding to the coast. The clouds were gone and the day was bright and hot. Gary and Mother sat in the dunes above the beach and watched me and Kabo walking at the water's edge, where the waves crashed and reached up the sand and died at our feet. The cool salty wind off the Gulf felt good and healthy in my face. The noise of the place tried to smother my thoughts, but they were too loud, beating in my head and chest . . . Gary was leaving. We were all leaving. I couldn't hear them, but I knew they were talking about it. I felt like I was sensing everything for the last time. I felt that nothing would ever matter again.

41

It was late afternoon when we started back to the farm. The sun hung low and tired over the scrub pines at the edge of the beach road. I slid down in my seat between them and felt the wind through the truck windows lick across my sunburned face. Mother had the radio dialed to a country station and it was the first time I'd heard her listen to music in a long time. I closed my eyes and leaned against Gary and started to drift off.

After a while I heard him speak softly to her. "He doesn't know where your parents live, does he?"

I didn't open my eyes. I didn't move.

"No," she said.

Even in sleep I sensed us approaching Fourmile. I felt the rhythm of the turns and the worn blacktop through the seat. I knew when the truck slowed that it was about to make a gentle swing into the driveway. I heard the tires go silent on the dirt and the breeze across my face was gone. The smell of the pasture slipped over us. Mother down-shifted and I started to open my eyes. Suddenly Gary jerked away from me.

I sat up and looked at him. He was turned and watching over his shoulder.

"Drive around back, Linda," he said.

"What?" she said.

I spun in my seat and looked through the rear glass. The big Dodge truck I'd seen get the tractor was turning in to the driveway.

Mother saw it in the rearview mirror at the same time.

"Step on it," he said firmly.

The Dodge was picking up speed, coming at us fast. Mother sped up and angled across the yard. I leaned forward and hung on to the dashboard.

"Don't slow down," Gary said. "Stop it in front of the back door, get out, and lock yourselves inside the house."

I was too busy holding on to think about anything. Gary leaned down and reached under the seat and pulled out the Beretta. The side of the house flashed by and Mother leaned the truck into a hard turn. I was slung against Gary and I heard him grunt as his arm was mashed into the armrest. We fishtailed and slid sideways past the back door. Mother slammed on the brakes and we skidded to a stop and the truck coughed and died.

"Get out!" he yelled.

I followed Mother out the driver's side and she grabbed me and pulled me around in front of her. I ran for the house and she came up behind me and fumbled through her keys. I heard the Dodge tearing around the side yard and Mother pressed against me like she wanted to push the door in. It seemed like she couldn't find the key. It was taking too long. Then I saw a flash of blue roar past us and slide side-ways, grass and dirt arcing into the air. The door gave and I fell inside and crawled across the floor. I rolled onto my back just in time to see Mother slam the deadbolt.

"We can't leave him out there!" I yelled.

A violent crash of metal and glass sounded outside and I heard men shouting. Mother ran to the phone and started dialing.

"Help him, Mother!"

She turned to me with the receiver pressed to her ear. "Get in your room, Foster! Get under your bed!"

I backed a few steps toward the hall and stopped.

"Go!" she screamed.

I ran into my room and opened my dresser drawer and dug deep under the clothes. I found the revolver and fell to the floor with it and slid under the bed. I lay pressed to the cool wood with my heart thumping against it. Shouts and footfalls came clearly through the still night. I hoped Kabo had gotten out of the truck.

"It's an emergency!" I heard her scream into the phone. "I need the police! 1504 County Road 7!"

"He's in the barn!" a man shouted from outside.

I heard her going through the drawers of the sideboard. "Where is it!" I heard her say.

I wasn't going to tell her and I wasn't going to give it to her.

I let go of the pistol and put my hands over my ears and squeezed my eyes shut. I saw my father's face, his eyes blinking at me from somewhere far back in the patchwork of sticks and leaves and blood. A sudden rush of panic bolted through me hot and sick.

I grabbed the pistol and scrambled out the other side of the bed, got to my knees, and looked out the window. I saw one of Dax's friends, the taller one, approaching the bay doors with a shotgun at his shoulder. The other, shorter and heavier friend was jogging around the back of the barn with a shotgun at his hip. My eyes darted to the left and I saw what remained of the farm truck, smashed and mangled before the Dodge. Then I saw Dax sitting in the passenger seat, craning his head to watch it all. His face was so swollen that it took me a moment to recognize him.

"Come on out, you son of a bitch!" the tall man yelled. He was stopped now, just before the bay doors, holding the barrel of the shotgun steady at the still interior. I lifted the window, brought up the revolver, and held it trembling before me. Then I heard Kabo barking from the pasture.

My eyes searched the darkness for him but saw nothing.

"Run, Kabo," I muttered.

"Burn it!" Dax yelled. "Get the gas out of the truck!"

"He can't have gotten in there that fast!" the tall man replied.

I held the pistol out and locked my elbows and peered down the sights at the tall man. The barrel was still shaking and I had to take a deep breath to steady my arms.

"Where the hell you *think* he went?" Dax continued. "He ain't a ghost."

"Is that his dog out there?"

"I don't know, but I wish it would shut up."

I began squeezing the trigger. The tall one hesitated, then started backing away. Then he lowered his gun, turned, and jogged to the truck bed. Meanwhile Dax was opening the passenger door, sliding out slowly like it pained him. I eased off the trigger and swung the barrel of the revolver toward the truck.

"Get your ass back in the truck," the tall man said.

"I'm gonna go make up with her," Dax replied. "You just do your job."

The tall man frowned and reached into the truck bed and came out with a jerry can of gasoline. He gave it a slight shake and turned and hurried away with it.

Dax approached the house door and I lost sight of him. I heard him try the knob and beat on it. "Open up, Linda!"

Kabo was still barking.

I swung the revolver back to the tall man. I tracked him as he uncapped the gas can and began pouring it on the outside of the barn. When it was empty he slung it across the yard. Then he reached in his pocket and pulled out a cigarette lighter. I took another breath and tried to steady my nerves.

"Get ready!" the tall man yelled. He touched the lighter to the wall and flicked it. The barn woofed into flame and he stumbled back with his hand over his eyes. I saw Kabo standing beyond the fence in the firelight.

Dax yelled again. "Open the damn door, Linda, before I kick it in!"

I heard Mother whimper. I swung the revolver toward the back door but Dax was still out of sight. The fire cracked and popped, licking up the boards and crawling over the hay. The yard appeared in shimmering orange light, the pecan orchard casting long shadows over the pasture.

Suddenly the short man fired and dirt leaped in Kabo's face. The dog spun and bolted toward the far trees.

"You hit it?" the tall one shouted.

"I don't think so. But I got it to shut up."

I looked back at Dax and then past him over the wrecked truck. Just where the shadows began something caught my eye. It might have been movement, but then I thought maybe it was just something out of place. Something only a person who'd lived at Fourmile for years would pick up. There was a fence post across the yard that nearly touched a pine tree. Nearly. There was always a gap. Now, there was no gap. And as the orange light flickered and reached this place, I thought I saw a hue of pale skin. I thought I saw a man standing there still as a marionette.

Wham! Dax hit the door with his shoulder and I felt the blow through the walls. He backed away into the grass and doubled over in pain.

The tall man distanced himself from the barn, swinging his shotgun from one side to the other. I still couldn't see the short man. The fire was growing bigger and louder, snapping and wheezing like a dragon.

"Damnit, Linda!" Dax shouted, straightening and rubbing his shoulder.

I turned back to the man in the shadows. For a brief instant, I saw Gary's face in the light. It seemed he was staring right at me, but I knew he was really looking at Dax.

"Cox!" the tall man yelled.

I didn't hear a response.

"No!" the tall man yelled again. "I don't know where else he'd be!"

Wham! I heard wood splinter and Mother scream. I knew Dax had kicked the door in. He backed away again and bent over with his hands on his knees, panting.

I saw the glint of the Beretta as Gary raised his left arm, smooth and mechanical.

He's right-handed, I thought. *He's going for the men with the guns first.*

A flash came from the barrel of the pistol. I didn't even hear the shot through the noise of the raging fire. The tall man spun and dropped the shotgun and seemed disoriented. Another flash came and the man dropped to his knees and rolled over. Gary's arm swung slightly to his left and the Beretta kicked and flashed twice more. I didn't see the short man, but I didn't doubt he got the same treatment. Mother screamed again. Dax was in the house.

"Hey, sweetheart," he said.

"I called the cops, Dax!"

"I'm sure you did. And it might just take a while for 'em to get out here . . . Where's the little head case?"

I stood and ran from my room into the hall. I saw him standing there. I leveled the pistol on his goat face and tightened my finger on the trigger. "Leave her alone!" I screamed.

He turned to me with a blank expression. His face was so black and blue and disfigured that it would have been hard for him to have any expression at all.

"Foster!" Mother yelled.

Dax smiled at me. It was an evil, pained smile. "You gonna shoot me, kid?"

"I will," I said. I felt the give in the trigger, my sweat on the steel.

"You're a pussy, kid. A momma's boy."

"Put it down, Foster," Mother said calmly.

"He taught me how to shoot it," I said. "And I liked fishing with him. And I loved him."

"He's dead. When are you gonna get your head around it?"

The metal sights came into view, blurry and aligned on his mouth. I shifted my feet and took a quick breath. I squeezed harder on the trigger.

42

Dax's head snapped back like he'd been slapped on the forehead with a board. He fell out of view. I hadn't fired a shot. Mother screamed something I didn't understand and I eased my finger off the trigger. Then I heard men grunting in the kitchen and I ran down the hall and turned the corner and would have kept going had Mother not grabbed my shirt and yanked me back. I saw Gary getting off the floor, dragging Dax by the hair with one arm. Dax tried to scramble to his feet, but Gary yanked him off balance and whipped him around like a doll.

"Gary!" Mother yelled. "The police are coming!"

Gary didn't answer. He didn't seem to realize we were there. Dax reached out and grabbed a cabinet door handle and Gary stopped and raised his boot and crushed the hand against the wood. Dax cursed in pain and rolled and flipped. Gary jerked him forward and slammed his head sideways into a cupboard. Dishes and coffee cups crashed down over them and shattered against the tile floor. Mother pulled me to her and put her arm around my neck and held me there. She didn't attempt to shield my eyes or turn me away. Both of us knew we couldn't say or do anything to stop what was happening. Neither of us wanted to turn away from it.

Dax cried for help as Gary dragged him out the door into the night.

Officer Tate was young and fidgety and didn't seem to know how to proceed. He kept his gun out and kept glancing at the windows. Officer Green, an older man, was outside walking around the house with two more policemen. Their cars were silently strobing blue and white across our yard.

"What's his name?" Officer Tate asked.

Mother seemed stunned and distant. "Gary," she replied.

"Gary what?"

"Conway."

"How old is he?"

Mother shook her head.

"About how old?"

"Twenty-five." Then she looked up at him and her eyes grew liquid like she'd gathered her wits for a moment and thought about it all. She said, "Christ."

"You want me to take the boy out and put him in the squad car? I mean, just to sit there while we talk?"

Mother shook her head.

Officer Tate studied her. "Okay," he said. "We know plenty about Dax Ganey and the Hadley brothers. What can you tell me about Gary Conway?"

"Not much," she said. "He was in the military. He has a dog."

"What branch of the military?"

"I'm not sure. He said Special Forces."

"That's all you know?"

Mother looked at me. "We have his dog tags," she said.

"I'll need you to bring 'em to me."

"Foster," she said.

I hesitated. There was no way. "You get them," I said.

Mother got the tags and brought them to Officer Tate. He was looking them over when Officer Green appeared at the back door. He was sweating and breathless. "Lord," he said. "They're out there, Tom. The Hadley boys. They crawled a little ways into the pasture, but they're shot up pretty good. Horace and Pete are keepin' an eye on 'em."

"They didn't give you any trouble?"

Officer Green shook his head. "They weren't armed. We didn't see their weapons."

"You all right?"

Officer Green wiped his face with the back of his hand. "Where's the fire trucks and ambulances?"

Officer Tate didn't have an answer. "She says he's Special Forces," he said. "I've got the dog tags right here."

The older man dropped his hand and lifted his eyebrows. "No kidding?"

Officer Tate held out the tags. "That's right."

"That explains it," Officer Green replied. "It's clean. Real clean. Two shoulders and two kneecaps. I guess he got their weapons too."

Officer Tate swallowed and shifted his feet. "You didn't see the others?"

"No," the older man said.

The younger one faced Mother again. "No vehicles left this place?"

She shook her head.

"And last you saw they were at that door?"

"Yes."

"Then they're still out there somewhere," the older one said. "Let's wait until more help gets here before we press it."

"Stay with these two while I go back out to the car and call in the social security number on this tag," Officer Tate said.

"He was protecting us," Mother said quickly.

"I heard you, ma'am. I've got it all written down."

While Officer Tate was outside, the older policeman had us sit on the sofa in the living room. Then he stood in the middle of the floor and watched us. In the distance I heard a river of sirens piercing the night.

"I don't think there's much they can do for that barn, ma'am."

"I understand," she said.

"But you don't want those sparks fallin' on your roof or settin' your pasture on fire."

Mother shook her head.

"You seem like a nice lady," he said. "If you don't mind me askin', how'd you get mixed up with Dax and them?"

"I don't know the Hadley brothers," she said. "I mean, I just met them once when they bought a tractor from us."

"If you know Dax well enough, then you ought to know Colby and Cox Hadley."

"I didn't know him well enough," Mother said.

"They've been runnin' together since they were teenagers. Into trouble most of the time."

Mother didn't answer.

Officer Green glanced at me, then faced Mother again. "This doesn't surprise me," he said.

The door opened and Officer Tate stepped inside. The sirens were louder now and seemed near to turning onto our driveway.

"They found two shotguns thrown into the pasture," Officer Tate said.

"The Hadleys'?"

"We think so. And Marcy got back to me on our mystery man. The guy's a deserter."

"Deserter?" Mother repeated.

"What's that?" I asked.

None of them looked at me.

"That's right," Officer Tate continued. "Left Virginia three months ago. Went home on leave, never reported back for duty."

"That's all?" Mother said.

"As far as we know."

Mother looked down and took a deep breath. The sirens ceased and I heard the groan of the big diesel engine as it downshifted in the driveway.

"What's a deserter?" I asked again.

"He left the military without permission," Officer Tate said.

Suddenly I knew what Mother was thinking. "But that's not bad," I said.

"He'll go to prison for it," the older policeman said.

"For how long?"

"I don't know," Officer Green said. "We're just supposed to arrest him and turn him over to the military. That kind of thing's handled by the Feds. And I don't know what they'll think about all this."

"I told you he was protecting us," Mother said.

"Whatever's goin' on out there now ain't self-defense,"

Officer Tate said. "But they've got a canine unit on the way. He won't get far."

I leaped from the sofa and rushed for the back door.

"Foster!" Mother yelled.

"Where's he goin'!" I heard Officer Green shout.

43

They might have yelled for me again, but all I heard was the roar of the fire engine as it charged along the side of the house like it would run me down. I circled wide around the heat and glow of the burning barn, covering my mouth against the ash swirling in my face. I kept on through the back gate where the air was clean and wet field grass slapped against my ankles and soaked my shoes. I heard men yelling and generators rumbling, but I had mostly wind in my ears. I kept my eyes focused on the wall of dark trees rising across the pasture. I tripped and rolled, got up, kept on.

The chaos of Fourmile fell behind me, but remained clear like something over a lake. Soon I heard a dog barking from down in the creek bottom. I kept on into the tree shadow and finally came up against the woods, before the old logging road. I stopped and caught my breath and stared at the darkness before me. Kabo sounded out of it like something through a culvert pipe. Gary had gone in there. It seemed everything I loved was sucked into that black hole.

"Gary," I said.

I stepped into the trees and a heavier darkness fell over me like a cloak. Kabo's barking wasn't far. Just beyond it I heard someone curse, then something crashing in the underbrush.

"Gary!" I called out.

Kabo grew silent, then I heard him running toward me through the broad gum leaves. A dark shadow rushed up and rubbed against my thigh. I reached down for him and he backed away and turned and barked in the direction of the creek. I grabbed his collar and he jerked me forward.

Kabo pulled me down the logging road, deeper into the bottom. I tripped along beside him until I sensed we were close to the ravine. Suddenly he stopped and whined at something ahead.

"Gary?" I said.

"Foster," he said through the darkness. His voice was strained like someone in a struggle. "You need to go back."

He was on the ground, not ten yards away, but it was too dark to make out anything.

"Gary, I—"

Dax suddenly screamed with desperation in a way that I'd never heard come from a man. Fear raced up my neck and I pulled Kabo back a step. I heard sticks breaking and more struggling in the leaves. Kabo barked furiously and strained at his collar like he would drag us both into the fight.

"Gary!" I yelled.

I heard the dull sound of meat getting punched, a groan, and all was still again. In the distance was the faint barking of police dogs.

"Get out of here, Foster," he said.

I didn't move.

"Take Kabo back into the field."

Dax mumbled something and there was another brief struggle. I heard the click of the hammer on the Beretta. All was still again. The canine unit was coming fast across the field.

"Get out of here, Foster," he said again.

"It doesn't help me, Gary."

Gary didn't respond right away. I heard Dax's raspy breathing like his throat was being squeezed.

"I'm in a fix, Foster," Gary finally said.

The dogs were close. I saw lights waving through the trees and heard voices.

"I wanted to see this through for you and your mother. Can you tell her that?"

"I want to come over there, Gary."

"Stay where you are."

"I can't see you, Gary. I'm scared of the dogs. I want to come over there."

"No! Don't move. Hold Kabo."

"Gary?"

A bright light passed overhead then jerked down and I saw Gary backed against a tree. He clamped Dax's head viselike in the crook of his knee, the other leg locked around the ankle in a triangle hold. He held his bad arm up to shield his eyes while the other fixed the Beretta to Dax's temple. Dax's eyes were wide and blinking like a goat caught by a python.

"Drop the gun!" a police officer yelled.

Gary slowly moved the Beretta away and dropped it into the leaves. I pulled Kabo to me and hugged him close around the neck. The German shepherds came past me, leaping against their body harnesses and digging their back legs into the damp soil. There was more shouting now from all the men behind them, but it was all too confusing to understand. Someone grabbed me and pulled me up.

"Come on, Foster," came Officer Tate's voice.

"Hands in the air!" someone yelled.

Gary held up both his hands and unclasped his legs so that Dax rolled away. Officer Tate pulled on me again. I turned just as Gary disappeared beneath the swarm of men.

44

Officer Tate grabbed my wrist with one hand and Kabo's collar with the other. Clamping his flashlight in his mouth, he hurried us out of the creek bottom. Once we stepped into the field again he stopped. The dogs behind us weren't barking as much and the men weren't shouting. Kabo was calmer and Officer Tate passed him back to me and took the flashlight from his mouth.

"You got him?"

"Yes," I said.

"Let's go, then."

It looked like a spaceship had landed on Fourmile with fire truck, ambulance, and police car lights blinking and flashing. The fire truck also had a floodlight that lit up the ground past even the back fence. The barn fire was out but the charred smell of it drifted over us.

As we drew closer I saw the black skeleton of the barn hissing and popping and smoldering. One ambulance had pulled away, but the firemen were still wetting the embers and the yard was alive with radios squawking and men shouting across the lawn at one another.

Mother was waiting for us at the back door.

"He's okay," Officer Tate said to her. "Go inside, Foster."

I expected her to wrap her arms around me, but she didn't. She acted distant and tired. She stared over the pasture and touched the top of my head as I passed. I walked Kabo through the kitchen and into the living room. Before I had time to sit, Office Green came through the front door. He saw me and took a deep breath. Then he looked over my shoulder at Mother.

"All right," he said. "Both of you sit down and don't move until we get everybody where they need to be."

I sat on the sofa and Kabo lay down at my feet and I released my hold on his collar. Another ambulance rushed past the window and continued toward the back field.

"You think they'll let us talk to Gary?" I asked her.

"I don't know," she said.

A few minutes later the posse came in from the pasture. The dogs were silent and all I heard was the jingling of their harnesses and footfalls. Kabo whined and started to stand, but I pressed him down. The men said a few words in the front yard and then I heard car doors shutting. I got up so I could see out the window.

"Foster," Mother said.

I stepped closer and tried to see Gary through the men and lights, but I couldn't.

Officer Green came through the front door again and saw me. "Sit down, kid."

"What happened to him?" I asked.

"He almost killed him," Officer Green said. "He's on the way to the hospital with the Hadley brothers."

"I meant Gary."

"*He's* okay. They've got him in the car out there."

"Can I talk to him?" I asked.

"He'll be at the Robertsdale jail. You can go talk to him there if you want."

It was close to eleven o'clock before Mother was through dealing with the policemen and firemen. We drove to the Robertsdale jail and the night clerk signed us in and escorted us down the hall to a steel door. He unlocked it and ushered us inside. "He's the only one in there," he said. "Go on in."

We entered a short hall with two cells. A big clock like the one in my classroom ticked loudly overhead. At the end of the room was a television that wasn't on. Gary sat on a cot in the far cell, slowly wiping his face with a washcloth. His arms were streaked with briar cuts. When he looked up at us, I saw his face was just as bad. Mother stopped and put her arm around my chest and pulled me to her.

"How are you?" she said to him.

He draped the washcloth over the end of the bed. "A little tired," he said.

"How's your arm?"

He glanced down at the dirt-smeared bandage. "Feels like it held under there," he said. "You did a good job."

They studied each other. Neither of them seemed to know what to say.

"You want me to get anything for you?" she finally asked.

He shook his head. After a moment Gary stood and came to the bars and held them like I'd seen in so many prison scenes. He was still looking at her when he said, "I'm fine, Linda. There's nothing left to do."

Her arm dropped from my chest and she slid past me and touched his hand and pulled away again. "I'm going to leave you with Foster," she said.

"Okay," he said.

He watched her go. Afterward I stood there looking at my shoes, listening to the clock ticking.

"Why'd you leave the army?" I asked.

"I got scared," he said.

I shook my head. "No you didn't."

"Yes, I did."

I swallowed back the tears.

"I was going to tell you about it," he said. "I was going to tell you why I had to go. I wanted you to know it wasn't anything you did. It wasn't anything you or your mother could have changed. I'd give anything for things to be different."

"Tell me everything's going to be okay, Gary."

"You just have to keep moving ahead. You'll make good decisions and you'll be a great boy and a great man. But you have to move on. You can't be afraid."

"How do I do that?"

"You go to Montgomery with your mother and you make your life there. The rest will be fine."

"How do you know, Gary?"

"Because I'm older than you. That's how I know."

"But we never got to go camping and I still haven't caught the fish—"

"Stop that, Foster."

I wiped my face with the back of my hand. "You're not my daddy," I said.

"I know I'm not."

I reached my arms through the bars of the cell and pressed my face against his chest and cried into his shirt. There was nothing left to say.

45

Gary was sentenced to six years in Leavenworth for desertion. All assault charges against him were dropped. After their conviction, Dax and the Hadley brothers were taken away to Holman State Prison, each of them carrying a life sentence for attempted murder.

The first few months Gary and I wrote each other every week. He didn't tell me much about what it was like in prison, mostly what he wanted to do when he got out. His plans never mentioned coming to see us. They were always about the Spanish gold and his ideas of how he might go about finding it. They were strange letters, more like he was talking to himself than to me. They didn't sound like the Gary I remembered.

Mother never spoke of him. She saw the letters come to me, but she never opened them and never asked me about them. I wrote back about Kabo, our house, my new school, friends, and the baseball team. There was a lot to tell, but, like Gary, I also had things I didn't want him to know. My letters grew less frequent and his shorter. As winter gave way to spring and baseball they had all but stopped.

Our new house was only a few blocks from Carlisle Middle School and the public park where we had our games. I impressed the coach enough to start most of the time and usually played next to Cory in the outfield. I also pitched relief if Blake, our first-string pitcher, wasn't there.

Grandmother passed away that winter and Granddaddy moved in with us. He came to all of my games and sat in the stands and studied our plays. He knew a lot more about baseball than he did about farming. As we walked home he'd give me a recap of the game and his encouragement and advice as to how we could improve.

In May we made the city playoffs and lost by just one run. We were all disappointed, but for the first time in years I felt a part of something bigger than me. The health of that feeling was stronger than any disappointment.

School let out for summer and I joined Cory and Blake and the other kids for daily baseball at the park. The first day I stood in the outfield, backed up close to the edge of the woods. The smell of cut grass sat heavy in the mid-morning heat and the sound of cicadas rose and fell behind me. The combination of these things took me back to Fourmile, painting the fence next to the blacktop, watching Gary walking toward me through the vapory air.

That night I wrote what would be my last letter to him. It was longer than usual. I told him about the playoff game and how close we'd come. I told him about the campout I'd had with the church youth group. Finally, I told him that he'd been right. Mother and I were happy in Montgomery. I sealed the letter and got up from the kitchen table and placed it on the counter. Kabo stood and got next to me and I reached down and scratched him behind the ears.

"Come on, boy," I said.

I never heard from Gary again and I was thankful for it. As much as he meant to me at Fourmile, he was the tail end of something terrible and beautiful that was too hurtful to parse out.

One day I'll drive past Fourmile to see if it looks as I remember it. To see the giant pecan tree standing alone at the edge of the orchard. To run my eyes over the pasture and search for that same thing Granddaddy was searching for in the old beach house. It doesn't scare me now. I know I'll see what he saw. I'll see nothing. I figured that out on my own. It had never really been about Fourmile at all. It was never about the place, it was about the memories. And I owned those memories and they never got left anywhere.